Touched by her Elven Magic

A Nocturne Falls Universe Story

Kira Nyte

TOUCHED BY HER ELVEN MAGIC
A Nocturne Falls Universe Story

Published in the United States of America.

Dear Reader,

Nocturne Falls has become a magical place for so many people, myself included. Over and over I've heard from you that it's a town you'd love to visit and even live in! I can tell you that writing the books is just as much fun for me.

With your enthusiasm for the series in mind – and your many requests for more books – the Nocturne Falls Universe was born. It's a project near and dear to my heart, and one I am very excited about.

I hope these new, guest-authored books will entertain and delight you. And best of all, I hope they allow you to discover some great new authors! (And if you like this book, be sure to check out the rest of the Nocturne Falls Universe offerings.)

For more information about the Nocturne Falls Universe, visit http://kristenpainter.com/sugar-skull-books/

In the meantime, happy reading!
Kristen Painter

Touched by her Elven Magic

Kalen Hawkins has only two goals—find help for his sister in Nocturne Falls and evade the evil genius hunting them. After almost a lifetime of captivity, he has little trust to spare, even for a sexy elf with a sweet heart and a galaxy of stars in her eyes.

Faunalyn "Fawn" Ayre loves the people and peculiarities of the small Georgia town where every day is Halloween. It's the perfect place for a nature elf to put down roots and live the life she's dreamed of—until a mysterious stranger literally crashes into her happy existence. She can't help but be drawn to the stunningly handsome man who is part fae, part... something else, and entirely too noble.

The last thing Kalen wants to do is draw Faunalyn into danger, but her loyalty and determination are impossible to resist. And she just may hold the key to his heart...and survival.

Website for Kira Nyte: www.kiranyte.com
Kira Nyte on Facebook: facebook.com/kiranyte
Kira on Twitter: @kiranyteauthor
Contact Kira Nyte at kiranyteauthor@gmail.com

Books by Kira Nyte

NOCTURNE FALLS UNIVERSE

A Dragon Speaks Her Name

A Dragon Gambles for His Girl

Merry & Bright, A Christmas Anthology
A Dragon's Christmas Mayhem (novella)

The Princess Protects Her Huntsman

SCIENCE FICTION / FANTASY ROMANCE

The Gala Lover

Chapter 1

Ribbons of steam wafted up from the street, the cool rain sizzling off the hot pavement. The first time he saw that a few days ago, it slowed him down.

Not tonight.

Even an hour after sunset, the sky draped in its navy blue cloak in preparation for the pitch of darkness, Georgia's temperature remained merciless. The damp coating on the roadway proved slick in areas, hampering the needed speed to reach his destination.

A strained groan from the passenger seat ramped up his urgency.

Kalen Hawkins reached over the console and squeezed his sister's knee. "Almost there, Vivi. Hang on just a little while longer."

His sister's small frame contorted beneath the black cloak. He caught a flash of fangs a moment before she hissed. Her body arched off the car seat, fingers biting hard into her thighs as she fought for control. Kalen pressed the accelerator closer to the floor. Closer to breakneck speed on this strange and curving forest road.

It had taken him three days to reach Georgia from the Canadian border. Three days of watching, helplessly, as his sister deteriorated beside him. Three days of realizing half of her genetic makeup was falling victim to both predator and invader. Half-vampire, half-fae, the Hawkins siblings were an anomaly, to say the least.

An anomaly that became a scientific pincushion in hopes of uncovering the secret that would allow vampires to become day walkers.

Whatever experiments were performed on Vivian in the week leading up to their escape only served to feed the vampire in her and quickly eat away at the fae.

Vivian's body jerked, twisting into a seemingly uncomfortable position. One hand found Kalen's wrist and squeezed, squeezed so hard his fingers began to tingle due to the lack of circulation. Her nails tore into his skin and he bled onto her pants.

The pain of the wound was nothing compared to the pain in his heart. He'd failed his sister, failed their mother, failed himself. He broke a promise to their father before he sacrificed himself to save his wife, his son, and his unborn daughter.

The screech-shriek-wail that exploded through the car lanced straight through his heart.

"Vivi, fight it. Please, fight it."

Please, goddess, give her strength.

She needed more than a prayer. She needed a damn miracle.

Dusk slipped into the hands of night. Kalen's vision cleared as the vampire in him took over. The foggy patches that obscured the lines in the road were as nothing to his new clarity. Everything, from the veins on the leaves of the forest trees to the scent of warm moisture filtering through the car vents became crystal clear.

Kalen pushed forward. He couldn't lose another day to the sunlight, even if he could deal with the discomfort the UV rays caused to his skin and his eyes.

When you get there, to Nocturne Falls, when you find my nephew, he'll know what to do. Don't let anyone know about your breeding. The fae is obvious to those who know what to look for, but the vampire in you must be kept hidden. Even in safety, there is danger. Dr. Hamstead will not stop his search until he has you back in his lab or he is dead.

Nicholas Tennerston's assurance and stern warning resonated in his mind. He was one of the six Lab Coats who observed him and his sister. He was the only one who showed emotion, from a twitch at the corner of his mouth to the sadness that softened his dark eyes.

Nicholas had been Kalen's mentor in life beyond the steel blue walls, the medical tables and chairs, and the merciless poking and prodding of instruments. He taught Kalen and Vivian hope and instilled in them a will to survive.

That same will kept Kalen hyper-focused on their destination, despite the curiosity that threatened to derail him.

The sports car's headlights reflected off a street sign unlike any other they passed since their escape. Even from a distance, the flash of the headlights on the reflective paint of the lettering made him narrow his eyes.

Welcome to Nocturne Falls. Where every day is Halloween.

His heart did a strange jump before slowing to its methodical thump…thump…thump. He gave Vivian's knee another squeeze.

"We've made it. We're here. Now, to find Jackson. We'll get you well in no time. Keep fighting, Vivi. Keep fighting," he said in a soothing voice, tempering the excitement he felt. Vivian's muscles were solid beneath his fingers, tension-hardened as she fought the monster that tried to consume her. "Almost there."

The BMW's navigation device sputtered out consecutive instructions once the two-lane road opened into what looked like a fairly large town. Not like any of those light-blazing *cities* they'd passed through. He saw where the street led into a bustling area of the town, but the female voice instructed him to drive away from the busy section. As much as his curiosity pleaded for him to investigate, the sight of his sister wracked by faint tremors kept him on course. A course along a sparsely-lit street leading into a hilly section lined with more trees.

"Once Jackson figures out how to cure you, we'll check out this town. Wouldn't that be nice? To see a town? I'm sure they have, um...that, uh..."

Kalen's brows creased. He couldn't even remember the name of the cold sweet treat his mother gave them when they were good. The last time he'd licked at the scoop, he'd been five, Vivian only two.

A day later, men in black clothing tore into their lives, ripping their mother from his small arms. Despite his strength, he couldn't fight half a dozen adult men. Not once they stabbed him with a needle and stole consciousness from him.

He woke in a small steel-walled room and into a nightmare. His new life for twenty-six years.

Vivian's scream jolted him from his rancid memories. He barely had a chance to throw his arm up between them before his sister's small body slammed into him with the force of a dozen grown men.

His head smacked against the window. His hands tore free of the wheel. He forgot the car as he fought Vivian's fangs snapping viciously at his neck, her beautiful silvery-blue eyes lost to an eerie red evil.

"Vivian! It's me, Kalen! Stop!"

Vivian snapped again, her sharp fangs sinking into his forearm and tearing through his skin. The pain was short-lived as his body worked to heal even as he bled. He managed to grab her slender shoulders and force her into her seat.

The car bounced. Hard.

Kalen turned back to the wheel.

"Now recalculating," the navigation lady said.

He tried to turn the wheel faster. Tried to slow the car down, but must have hit the wrong pedal. It lurched forward.

"Three days isn't *enough*," he groused, bracing himself and his feral sister for impact.

"Oh, dear spirits!"

Faunalyn Ayre watched the scene unfold as if in slow motion. Dual headlights drew closer and closer, bouncing as the car swerved off the road. The black sports car barreling down the small hill at a ridiculous speed. Those lights nearly blinding her as she stood, shocked, just within the tree line. The distinctive *crunch-sizzle-whoof* as the car slammed into a tree only a handful of feet to her left.

A headlight popped and extinguished. Steam rose from beneath the crumpled hood and mangled grille.

Seconds ticked by before she blinked, gained her bearings, and rushed toward the car. A thin haze of dust and particles from the airbags and dash obstructed her view, but no one made a move to escape the car.

Until she reached the driver's side.

Hand on the handle, she caught a blur of color and movement before something plowed into her with the force of a semi.

Her back and head smacked into an old oak.

A man shouted, "Vivian!"

Struck by a detached calm, Fawn managed to wedge her hands between herself and the cloaked beast clawing at her shoulders. A rush of heat flowed up from her feet, legs, torso, down her arms, and expelled out through her fingertips.

Instantly, her attacker's body slackened, crumpling to her feet in a black hump of cloth.

Fawn's attention shot to the man sprinting toward them. Stunning eyes shifted between herself and the heap on the ground, which shuddered with soft sobs. Fawn shook off the earthen power that had subdued her fear and dropped to her knees.

"Don't! Don't touch..."

Fawn drew back the hood of the cloak and stared at a terrified young woman, face streaked with tears. Pale hair clung to her cheeks and her eyes glowed almost...purple.

"Are you okay?" Fawn asked quietly, acutely aware of the man falling to his knees across from her. His terrified essence was toxic, but the heat of his presence was oddly...soothing.

The woman grabbed her wrist. "Help...me."

Fawn's eyes went again to the man. Her first inclination was to believe he was the threat, but her instincts protested vehemently. She was half stunned when the woman rested her head on her lap, one small hand clinging to Fawn's wrist as if for dear life.

Any tighter and the stranger might sever Fawn's hand from her arm.

Still, she couldn't bring herself to tear her gaze from the breathtaking...male creature—there was no way the man was anything close to mortal. He was dressed in black, and wore the color exceedingly well. A T-shirt, jeans, boots. His ash-blond hair was longer than most men wore it, brushing the bottoms of his ears and falling over his cheeks to reveal bluntly tapered ears.

Fawn felt her head tilt, though she didn't consciously move.

His face was beautiful. Eloquent and sharp and on the pale side, like some of the vampires she knew from town. Even his lithe build reminded her of a vampire, but that blood-lust vibe didn't pulse off him the way it did others.

Then, there were his eyes. A shocking silver-blue that appeared to shimmer in the darkness. The color resonated with icy waters or crushed aquamarine spattered with diamonds. It should have chilled when all it did was warm.

Magic. Those eyes were magic. A magic she was distantly familiar with.

Her assessment took no more than seconds, right down to the certainty that he remained unharmed from the accident. Not a single cut, scrape, or bruise marred his gorgeous face.

Fawn glanced down at the woman. Her eyes were closed, but tears streamed silently down pale cheeks. Faun urged magic from the Earth to flow over the woman in search of injuries.

"Vivian, is it?" she asked, recalling the man's bellow. She ran the tip of her finger over the woman's brow, ignoring the man's burning gaze. He wanted to take this woman away from her, but something held him back. Something she couldn't pinpoint, and she suspected he couldn't either. "Were you hurt in the accident?"

A minute shake of the woman's head.

"I need to get her out of here," the man finally said. His voice was hitched with urgency, but it couldn't quench the deep fluid richness. Did he speak with an accent? She couldn't be sure, but he definitely wasn't from around here.

Stricken by his appeal, she almost let him take the woman.

As his arms hooked beneath the woman's back and legs, the woman's hand tightened on Fawn's wrist. Fawn shook her head and tugged the woman closer. "No. You're not going anywhere. Can't you see she's terrified of you?"

The man's head shot up, his eyes wide and those full lips agape.

Fawn shook her head again, this time with more conviction. "Absolutely *not*."

"You don't understand. I have to—"

"I think it's *you* who doesn't understand. She ran from a wrecked car and asked me to help her. She ran *from* you." Fawn wrapped a protective arm around the woman's back and tugged her closer. "I'm calling the sheriff. You—"

The man yanked back his arms and threw up his hands. A surge of icy fear pummeled her. *His* fear.

"No."

She had no idea how she could feel his emotions so strongly. She suspected it had something to do with those ears of his, but he simply didn't jive with elfishness. She would know. She was an elf.

The man raked both hands through his hair.

That's when she saw it. The association and the paradox.

Fangs.

Barely extended, but notable nonetheless.

Fawn's body weakened. She looked at the woman. Her lips parted as she breathed, the tiny tips of fangs barely visible. How had she missed those?

"Sweet spirits of the Earth, *what are you*?" she whispered.

In her moment of confusion, the man snatched the woman out of Fawn's arms and was on his feet before she could blink. He was halfway up the hill by the time she got to her feet, and at the roadside by the time she ran to catch up with him.

"Wait! You were just in a car accident. You can't leave the scene until the sheriff's deputies show up—"

"No...*deputies*." The man spoke the last word like it was poison on his tongue. He spun on her, his eyes narrowed. "I must find help."

"Okay." She raised her hands in a motion of peace. "Okay. But first, are you hurt? Do you need to go to the hospital?"

A bolt of fierce hatred shot through the man's eyes and burned along her skin. He was either awfully powerful, or he was untrained in controlling his emotions. The extremes were unnerving.

Her attention drifted to the woman when her small hand lifted to the man's chest.

Don't go daydreaming, Fawn. He's got a lady.

The man's hardened expression cracked as he looked down into the woman's face, half-hidden by the cloak's hood. Fawn could almost hear him shatter as an overwhelming pulse of love rolled off him. Warmth crept up her neck and she lowered her arms, and her gaze. She didn't need to intrude on this awkwardly tender moment.

"Let her help," the woman said, so softly Fawn could barely make out the words.

The man's lips tightened. When he spoke, his accent thickened and his voice rolled in a sensual rumble that made absolutely no sense.

Fawn stiffened.

Well, it did make sense, but it shouldn't. Not from his tongue. Not with that much power.

It simply solidified her curiosity about this couple.

The street lightened in warning of a car's approaching headlights. Fawn cleared her throat. The man looked at her through narrowed eyes. She reached for his arm—oh, dear goddess, were those sparks running up her fingers?—and hurried him away from the roadside.

Bad static electricity. From grass.

"Come on. You're going to draw attention to yourself by standing here with a woman in your arms." She jabbed a finger in the air toward the crumpled car. "Like that isn't going to do the job anyhow. Hurry."

She'd worry about the sparks later. Right now, if she was going to help them, she needed to get them out of sight. The car would just have to wait.

Chapter 2

Kalen didn't want to *feel* anything toward anyone other than Vivian. He'd dedicated his life to protecting her the best he could under their circumstances. Nothing else mattered, not even the breath in his lungs, as long as Vivian was safe.

But when the Lab Coats had restrained him and stole her away during their lunch in the atrium that fateful day, his breath had frozen until his chest was consumed by sharp agony.

He realized then, even before they began the tests, that he had failed.

Nicholas educated him about trust, and warned him of its deception.

Trust must be earned, Kalen. It is not something you give freely. It is something that one must show is deserved of you. And in turn, understand that you must show you are deserving of another's trust. But, be warned. Trust in the wrong hands can be lethal to you.

His beloved sister *trusted* him to protect her and her trust was misplaced. Now, he had to earn that back. He would. He made a vow.

But…the stranger?

He followed her more on instinct. Her urgency to move away from the street matched his and set his feet in motion. Everything else about her set his eyes, and the strange thrumming beneath his skin, in motion. It was new and alien, both unsettling and delightful.

Sensations. Sensations he could not name, did not understand, but desperately wanted more of. Even if walking grew more uncomfortable with each second that passed.

A small sliver of guilt wedged into his mind. When he needed to find Jackson, he found himself distracted by the shear loveliness of this stranger. She was smaller, maybe only a few hairs taller than Vivian. Slender, but shapely. Her hair was the color of spun gold. He knew because Nicholas would sneak him videos and movies to educate him about the outside world. The woman's hair was the color of the melted precious metal, and shone in the night despite being tied up in something strangely messy yet pretty on top of her head. Her eyes, a lovely lavender and gold, ebbed calm into his otherwise panicked spirit. Soft curves and angles formed a beautiful face.

There was a serenity about her, one that instantly connected with him, although the logistics were lost to him. There was also an air of…trust.

As they hurried deeper into the forest, he hoped the trust he felt wasn't due to the *other* things that consumed his body.

He stole a quick glance over his shoulder. Through the trees, he could see a car had stopped on the side of the road. Someone had climbed out and was making the descent to the smoking sports car. A light glowed at the man's ear from a…cell phone was it?

"Hurry up," the woman urged.

Kalen didn't look back again. He estimated they walked about ten minutes more before he caught the soft yellow glow of a light. A few more minutes and they approached a small house set in the middle of an equally small clearing. Gardens surrounded the house, awash with splashes of colors he could see clearly in the dark. Their sweet scents made him slow. Vivian's head lifted long enough to look around, brows furrowed and nostrils flared. He caught the small smile crest her mouth before she tucked her head back into his chest.

"Pretty," she murmured.

His arms tightened in a mock hug.

"The girl," she whispered.

He stumbled. The woman paused and spun around.

"Are you okay?" she asked. Kalen nodded once. "Are you certain you don't need medical attention?"

Medical attention never led to anything good. He scowled before he could refrain from the action.

"No." He came up beside the woman. "No medical attention." He scrutinized the small house, listening for someone lying in wait. "Who lives here?"

The woman's sloped brows arched. "Me." She continued to the front door and pushed it open. "It's not a Hilton, but it'll do. I'm sure a deputy will be paying me a visit in the near future regarding the wreck, so"—she motioned for him to go inside—"make yourselves at home for now. Are you hungry? Thirsty?"

Why did his eyes go straight to her mouth when she asked those questions?

"No."

His answer came out more curtly than he anticipated. The woman's gaze lingered, making him uncomfortable in his skin. She finally beckoned him again off the single-step porch and into a cozy living space.

She closed and locked the door. The resounding *click* sent him into a subtle panic. His body stiffened and his senses honed in on everything around him. The sounds, smells, sights. The energy that flowed in the air.

The woman watched him like one of the Lab Coats back at the facility, eyes narrowed, pupils dilated, her expression all but masked. He sensed her tension, smelled the faint acridity of fear and doubt as she rounded a counter-like protrusion from the wall that led into what he recalled to be a kitchen. His room held no kitchen. He and his sister were served their meals in one of three places. Kitchen was not one of them. Neither was the *dining room.*

He did not know what to make of this freedom.

Focus on Vivi.

He turned his attention back to his sister, who dozed lightly in his arms.

"Don't look at me like that," he groused to the woman as he searched the small area for a place to set Vivian down.

Turning his back to the stranger, he tested a sofa, found it far more plush than the ones they had at the lab, and gently settled his sister on it. The woman's probing gaze continued to burn a line along his spine as it lit other places inside him on unwanted fire.

He tracked the woman's movements by the sound of her soft footsteps. When she approached, he twisted to face her, placing his body between the stranger and his sister. There was nothing malevolent about the woman, but his natural instinct to shield his sister held strong.

The woman held out a glass. "Iced tea. Homemade. I brew it from my own leaves and herbs." She took a sip from a similar glass, her pretty eyes never leaving his face. Kalen eyed the glass suspiciously, making no move to reach for it. "You must be thirsty. If anything, it'll help calm your panic and ease your mind."

Kalen hesitated, but finally flicked his hand toward the glass at her lips. "That one."

The woman finished her sip and glanced at her glass. She held both out for him. "Here. They're the same, I assure you. I didn't poison one. That's not in my nature."

The open door he hadn't realized he waited for. With hands on the glasses, he narrowed his eyes on the woman. "And *what* nature is that?"

The corner of his mouth twitched when she licked iced tea from her lips. He quickly lifted one glass to his nose, then the other, and smelled the brew. No differences that he could detect. No chemical additives or hints that she had poisoned his glass. Still, he took her glass and handed back the one she'd offered him. He didn't know this woman and certainly didn't *trust* her not to sedate him.

"I should ask you the same," she responded, drinking from the glass without hesitation. "What's your name?"

Kalen watched her for a long, hard moment, then turned back to his sister. He knelt on the floor beside the sofa as guard, and took a sip of the iced tea. It took a great deal of strength not to show his surprise as he tasted its delicious flavors. His second sip was deeper. He'd never tasted something so…amazing.

The woman took a seat in a plush chair adjacent to the sofa. "My name is Faunalyn Ayre. This is my home. I have a shop off Main Street where I sell smoothies and healthy fruit and granola bowls. Are you from around here?"

Kalen drank his tea, giving nothing away. His attention moved between Vivian and the stranger—Faunalyn—as he tried to process his body's reaction to the woman.

His senses were overwhelmed. Both vampire and fae. For the first time in three days, he almost wanted to run back to the safety of his quiet, plain room at the lab. The real world overstimulated him, causing his skin to tingle and his heart to race. He could barely perceive anything of Faunalyn through his own rush of sensations.

Faunalyn tried again. "Do you speak much English? I noticed you spoke a different language to your girlfriend." His lips tightened at her reference. A light pink colored the woman's cheeks and she began tapping the glass with her fingers. "Wife?"

"Sister," Kalen corrected. "She's my sister and I speak fine English."

The color in Faunalyn's cheeks deepened. She reached to the back of her neck and rubbed, tipping her head one way, then the other. He continued to stare, listening to the quickening of her heartbeat. He could smell a faint underlying saltiness a moment before he caught a glistening bead at her temple. His eyes lowered to the smooth expanse of skin at her neck, that sweet area where her carotid pulsed.

Nervous. She was nervous.

Well, that made two of them. His reasons far surpassed hers, he'd bet.

He lowered his head and fought back his fangs.

"You said a deputy would come here." Kalen diverted his attention from the woman and brushed the hair from his sister's cheek, tucking the pale strands behind her ear. Her heart had slowed to a beat every few seconds. Her breaths all but ceased. The vampire took over in sleep, but left Vivian to rest in peace. "When?"

The shift of cloth was his only clue to the woman's shrug. "Since your car was noticed wrapped haphazardly around a tree on my property, I'm sure it'll be sooner rather than later. The sheriff of Nocturne Falls, Hank Merrow, knows I enjoy walking the perimeter at dusk."

"Why?"

"Why does he know? Or why do I walk?"

"Both."

Did it really matter? He couldn't associate with anyone but Jackson. Not until they had cured Vivian and exposed the lab to…someone. Nicholas never told them what to do after Vivian was saved.

Would anyone listen to them?

"Because he is a friend and because I enjoy the space of time right before night takes over. There's magic in those precious moments and I like to bask in it."

He cocked his head, taking a better look at Faunalyn. "What do you know of magic?"

Her warm eyes cooled. "Remember you're in my home, sir. Respect me, and my space."

Sir. No one called him *sir.* He wasn't sure what to make of it.

Faunalyn rested her half-empty glass on the table between them. "Is there a place you're going? Someone you'd like to call? I can let you use my phone."

"You ask many questions."

The woman's shoulders straightened and her plump lips thinned, along with her unwavering serenity from a few moments earlier. "You don't seem to have many answers. Or a name." She pressed to her feet and crossed back to the kitchen. "People who hide names hide bad secrets."

"Where are you going?"

"This is my home. I'll go where I please."

Lights rolled down the wall in front of him. He jumped to his feet and spun to the window. Through the gauzy curtains, he saw the police car cruise down the driveway toward the house. A strobe of blue and white lights flashed through the thick cover of trees.

"Ah. I told you it wouldn't take long. If you don't want to provide answers, you might want..."

Vivian was in his arms before Faunalyn started talking. Her voice faded as he rushed to the back of the house, found a door, and escaped silently into the night. He didn't slow his sprint, leaving the house a memory and the lights nothing but a fading nuisance at his back.

He ran, keeping to the forests and the hills. He ran, following mental directions Nicholas showed him before the ambush. He ran until his feet brought him to a sliding glass door.

Kalen knocked, tracing the dim light pouring from a room down a hallway. When no one answered, he knocked again, more sharply.

"Why did we leave the woman's home?" Vivian asked, voice threaded with fatigue.

"It wasn't safe. She was asking too many questions. Nicholas told us to stay hidden and be as discrete as possible. To trust no one except for Jackson."

He wasn't going to go into detail about the other reasons he felt it necessary to leave. The cops and his body's uncharacteristic reaction to the woman were none of Vivian's concern.

He heard footsteps before he caught sight of the shadow moving across the floor. A moment later, a young man appeared on the other side of the glass, his hair tousled and glasses resting unevenly on his nose. Dressed in rumpled flannel pants and a T-shirt, the man looked entirely unprepossessing. Kalen wondered at Nicholas's expectations.

Had he gotten the address wrong?

The man rubbed his eyes, covered his mouth as he yawned, and squinted.

Kalen stepped back, prepared to race away with his sister.

Abruptly the man gasped, fumbled with the lock, and yanked the door open. "I-I'm sorry. I fell asleep. Come in. I've been waiting for you to arrive."

"Jackson?" Kalen asked.

The man nodded jerkily. "Of course."

Only a small beat of anxiety melted away as Kalen stepped through the door and into another strange house. Jackson spent a bit of time observing Vivian, which didn't sit well with Kalen.

"I kinda expected you to use the front door, but hey. Either way is fine. Did you find the place okay?"

The man stood a whole head shorter than Kalen, but there was no denying the shocking resemblance to Nicholas, right down to the wire-rimmed glasses.

"We had an accident, so we're without a car."

"Oh. That's not good. Are you both okay?" He cleared his throat. "Well, I mean, I'm sure you are, but..."

"We're fine. A young woman helped before we took our leave."

"Cops?"

Kalen shrugged. "We left before they saw us."

"Well, okay. Guess we'll just have to figure that one out when the problem arises. I'm sure Uncle Nick will have a solution." The man rubbed his forehead as he glanced over Kalen's shoulder. "Speaking of, where is my uncle?"

Kalen waited as the man leaned out the door and looked around the yard. As Jackson straightened and closed the door, the weight of their escape finally crashed down on Kalen's shoulders.

The young man blinked up at him. That small motion, along with the question in his gray eyes and the dense dread making its way into his essence, broke Kalen's resolve.

He sighed and shook his head as guilt threatened to take root in his heart. "I'm sorry. Nicholas is dead."

Chapter 3

"You look like you battled a storm the last few days."

Fawn laughed at Wendy, one of the two teenagers she had hired as an extra set of hands after school. The girl, seventeen and excited to be heading to college and away from her overbearing—according to her—parents in a year, tossed her cross-body bag onto an empty chair in the office. She shook out her hat—a dark purple baseball cap with Magical Mayhem Smoothies and More etched in a fun gold font—and tugged it over her short brown hair. Today's makeup of choice consisted of spirals of silver and gold leading from the corners of soft brown eyes and star gems strategically placed within those spirals.

"Don't you look pretty today. Any after-work plans?" Fawn asked, hoping to derail the sharp girl.

Wendy shrugged. "Braydon might stop by for a shake after he plays ball with a few friends. You know, he's caught the eye of a few recruiters from different universities. He's gonna make it big in the NFL one day."

Fawn lifted her chin and offered a half-grin. "I don't doubt it. He's a bear on the field."

Wendy pointed to her eyes. "No offense, Fawn, but you look like you didn't sleep a wink. Want me to touch you up? I have some fun colors in my bag. Oh! I like those new cuffs on your ears. But really. I'll do the makeup thing."

"Figured I'd go big with the bling today. You know." Fawn scrunched her nose and made a circular motion with a finger at her face. "To hide the stormy appearance. I'll pass on the makeup, but thanks. I need to get back out front. Come on out when you're ready."

"I'll be a minute."

Fawn slipped through the office door into the backroom and grabbed more cups and lids to restock. It was downtime, perfect for grabbing a bite and preparing for the early evening rush.

Only, her usual pep fled her and her mind kept rolling back to the strange couple from three nights ago. She never heard them leave. One minute, they were in the living room, woman asleep, man being stubborn and cocky, the next, poof! Gone. She had it in her mind to tell the deputy about the driver and the passenger of the car, but when Alex asked if she saw anything or if anyone sought help around the time of the accident, she denied everything. A breath of a voice fed her words while her memories flashed with images of that BMW speeding toward the tree.

She had no idea who the two were or *what* they were. The man's shuttered expressions and implacable silence assured her she wasn't going to find out. They were phantoms. They came, had tea, and left, never to be heard from again. Their entry into her life was sudden and short and had her questioning whether it had been a dream.

No matter how hard she tried, she couldn't shake thoughts of the man from her head, and that was confirmation enough that the couple was real. Every time she thought of him, her body hummed and stirred awake until she found an excuse to step into the walk-in fridge to cool down until her teeth chattered.

"The faster you forget him, the better off your sanity will be," Fawn muttered.

"What?" Wendy asked, stepping up beside her. "Sanity talk is never a good thing."

"Oh, nothing." Fawn forced a laugh as she opened the new stacks of cups and placed them on their respective piles. "I think I have deer eating my tomatoes."

"That can drive anyone crazy." Wendy leaned close, her arm against Fawn's, stopping the older woman's tidying. When Fawn glanced at the girl, she recognized the mischievous glint in her eyes and the teasing grin. "But you said *him*. If it's a guy, I can always tell him a thing or two. Anything to stand up for my best elf friend."

Fawn rolled her eyes to the ceiling. "You and your cursed panther hearing."

Wendy clicked her tongue. "Pays off."

"Well, if there's anything to tell, you'll be the first to know. Alas, there is nothing to tell, no sanity that will be lost over a participant of the male race, and no words to be had." Fawn handed Wendy the package of lids. "Mind putting these away while I grab more strawberries?"

"Sure. Oh, and might as well grab blueberries, too. I noticed there was only a package left in the fridge. Was going to grab them, but wanted to do inventory first."

Fawn gave Wendy a thumb's up and an exaggerated smile before escaping into the walk-in fridge. She gathered her fruit, an extra bag of granola she had made earlier that day, and oats.

When she returned to the front, a half-dozen customers had trekked into the store. Most gazed over the menu hanging on the wall behind the counter.

"How's the Spirit Soother?" one young lady asked. Wendy, all smiles and the perfect hostess, started her spiel.

"The chamomile-infused ice really adds a dose of calm to the drink. The flavor is mellow, but delicious. Give me a moment and I'll whip up a sample for you."

"Thanks!"

Wendy turned away from the crowd and prepared a blender with ingredients while Fawn washed the fruits and sorted them in their respectful containers. Most of the ingredients she used in her smoothies and fruit bowls she grew herself, but as the demand for her product exploded, she couldn't grow fruits and herbs fast enough on her little plot of land. She resorted to wholesalers she knew personally, whose products she trusted could be guaranteed as organic and the best the market had to offer.

Pretty much, they had to match up to what she could grow. There were very few of those suppliers around. Like...two. One was owned by a nature elf, like herself.

The shop, as always, got busy right before dinnertime, and the shift in weather from overcast to rain brought the customers in droves. The hustle kept Fawn and Wendy on their toes. Fawn broke a sweat half an hour into scooping and blending and preparing and taking orders, but she and Wendy worked like a well-paired team. They might have ten years between them, but they were the equivalent of sisters.

So when a new ribbon of warmth spread up her back, she thought nothing of it. Sweat already trickled down her spine.

"Catch, Fawn!" Wendy called from across the way. Fawn readied two metal mixing cups and began theatrically catching lobbed pieces of fruit for two smoothie orders while entertaining their crowd. She enlisted a small dose of magic for fun, causing the fruits to weave between each other as they arced through the air.

"Head's up, Wendy."

As Fawn caught the last of the dancing fruit, she tossed one cup to her employee and finished topping off the cup she held with the final ingredients before dumping everything into a blender and setting the speed.

When the second blender resounded through the shop, a loud round of applause erupted, some whistles and hoots mixed into the roar.

Fawn and Wendy laughed as they turned to their customers and bowed.

"And that's magical mayhem for you," Fawn told the crowd.

Her smile grew as she soaked in the excitement from the children and the awe of the adults. As with many tourists who visited Nocturne Falls, half of her customers were dressed in costumes that ranged from ghosts to witches to no-named things. Most were damp from braving the rain, but it didn't put a damper on their joy.

The blender stopped, signaling a completed smoothie. Fawn started to turn back to her work when a dark-clad figure seated at a table in the far corner at the front of the shop caught her attention. It took her only a moment to realize who he was. Although covered in a black hooded windbreaker and dark sunglasses absurdly perched on his nose, she could never mistake the face of perfection from three nights ago.

That warmth creeping up her back jacked up to scalding and poured over her like boiling water. Merciless and painful...in a pleasantly twisted way. She had the impulse to march over and demand he leave, but something in his presence, whether it was the way he tried to hide in plain sight or the sallow shadows that touched his otherwise beautifully structured cheeks, kept her from kicking him out.

The fun in her work snuffed, Fawn twisted back to the blender and poured the smoothie into a cup. She handed it to the waiting customer, accepted payment and a hefty tip, and took a few more orders. Her attention kept slipping to the man who didn't move from the table.

She worked beneath his watchful observation for an hour, unable to find her groove. It drew Wendy's attention more than once. They performed twice more for customers, both times her chosen magical displays nearly fumbling.

Wendy sidled beside her, her voice low. "You okay?" The crowd had thinned, leaving only a handful of customers.

And her new stalking shadow man.

Fawn sighed as she finished slicing bananas. The knife slipped and nicked the side of her fingertip. Blood welled from the cut and she groaned, instinctively popping her finger into her mouth.

"Hey, I'll handle this. You go fix that up before your Bleeding Heart smoothie turns literal. When you come back, you can tell me what's going on."

"Thanks."

Leaving her station, Fawn disappeared into the safety of the back room and headed straight to the First Aid kit next to the back sink.

A wisp of air ruffled her hair.

She gasped when the black-clad man appeared directly in front of her.

"What on earth are you doing back here?" she hissed, glancing over her shoulder at the doorway leading to the front of her shop. Unless Wendy poked her head back, Fawn and the man wouldn't be seen.

He grabbed her hand in a firm grip. "May I?"

"May you what?"

"*Help* you."

Fawn tried to say something, but her head nodded once of its own accord. She watched as the man brought her bleeding finger to his lips. His sunglasses did little to hide the intensity of his gaze as he sealed his lips against her finger.

This is…awkward and…wow.

She knew she needed to yank her hand away. What stranger appeared like a ghost to lick bleeding fingers?

The tip of his tongue flicked over the stinging cut.

I'm going to take my hand back. I will. She stared at him, sickly fascinated by his actions as her spine turned to liquid nerves that sputtered and sparked. *Annny moment now.*

The man lowered their hands, his thumb brushing over her damp finger. It took a long moment for her brain to register the lack of burn from her cut, but no time at all to swim in the burn this damn man lit everywhere else.

A glance at her finger showed unmarred skin. No cut. No blood. Nothing but intact flesh.

"Kalen Hawkins," he murmured, lifting his free hand to the side of her head. His fingers barely brushed over the tip of her ear. "My name. Kalen Hawkins."

She blinked. Glanced at the doorway between the front of the store and the back. Between normal and routine to strange and unusual. She had the sudden sensation of stepping into an alternate universe.

"Okay, Kalen Hawkins. That doesn't answer my question." She struggled to snap her awareness back to reality. It wasn't every day a hot creature showed up to heal her cuts with a lick. "What are you doing back here?"

She wasn't sure if she should thank him or yell at him for his play at doctor.

"I would like to talk to you."

Fawn's brows shot up. "Oh? *Now* you want to talk? Sharing your name is a peace offering, is it?"

"I...came by information and was told you were of sound character."

She was so not hearing this right. "And who are you to judge me? What are your sources?"

She shouldered past Kalen and stepped up to the sink. The blasted man-creature followed, keeping close at her back. If she wasn't confused by him, she might have actually enjoyed his close proximity.

She turned the water to cold and started washing her hands. "If I recall, you are a judgmental kind of..." She threw him a glance. "Whatever you are. And if you licked my bloody finger to satiate some wonky fetish, I forbid you to do it again."

Shutting off the water, she flicked droplets from her fingers before opening the First Aid kit to retrieve a Band-Aid.

"Why do you need a bandage?" he asked. "You have no cut."

"Because I don't have magical powers to heal a cut in less than five minutes and I have an exceedingly astute employee who'll notice there is no cut." She squeezed her eyes shut, gave her head a sharp shake, and spun to Kalen. "Listen, I don't owe you any answers or explanations after your rude behavior the other night. I think you'd be wasting your time hanging around my shop—"

"I would like to speak with you." Kalen reached for his sunglasses and pushed them up on his head. His stunning eyes softened the sharp edges of her frustration, breaking her down. Within the strange, hypnotic aquamarine and diamond shards, she saw something that brought out the nurturer in her. Desperation. "Please, Faunalyn."

"It's Fawn." The way her full name rumbled from his throat and dripped off his tongue was too enticing and sensual. She didn't like it. Oh, heck, she liked it *too* much. "You answer me this first. What are you? Because you're not just one paranormal race."

"No. I'm not." His voice lowered until she had to lean closer to hear him. "It is why I would like to speak with you. Jackson said you could be trusted."

"Jackson...?"

"Not here. Your *astute* employee can hear very well for a panther."

Fawn's back shocked straight. She instantly regretted the jerky motion when the front of her body brushed against Kalen's. Her face flushed beneath the sudden turn in his watchful eyes. From desperation and pleading to carnal. His pupils drank up the blue waters of his irises, and a sharp inhale flared his nostrils. The shadows along his cheeks shifted with the clench of his jaw.

They stood way too close and yet neither moved away.

"H-how do you"—she cleared the ball from her throat, only to have it settle lower, making it more difficult to speak—"do you know she's..."

A faint gasp escaped her as the tips of his fingers drew along her cheekbone, down to her mouth, and lingered on her lower lip.

"I know many things, and yet, so little."

Did he lean closer to her? Was that even possible?

Yes. Yes it is.

The surge of desire that swelled through her promised that.

"Please. I beg you. Speak with me. If not for me, then for my sister." He spoke barely above a whisper and yet his voice filled every inch of her head. Not telepathy, like some paranormals were capable of, but as if the enormity of his presence alone drowned her every sense.

In the end, through the thick veil of carnality that took over his expression and his tender touch, his desperation broke through poorly patched fissures of his resolve. His pain and worry resonated along her spirit, a darkness she could not ignore.

"Okay. I close up shop at nine. There's a parking lot behind the building. Meet me there. Nine-thirty."

Kalen nodded once, leaned down and...

No he did not.

She had no chance to catch a last glimpse of the strange man. He was gone the moment his lips left her forehead, the whisper of air across her skin cool where his mouth had touched.

Chapter 4

Fawn gave the okay for Wendy to leave with her boyfriend at eight and started the arduous process of cleaning up the shop. A few more customers trickled in for dessert smoothies, and it took every ounce of willpower for Fawn to plaster a smile to her face and wipe the image of Kalen from her head long enough not to screw up the orders. She suffered the resonance of his unexpected kiss the rest of the night, which was more curse than blessing.

As she came out of the walk-in from putting fruit away, she caught sight of Ivy Merrow and Charlie peering through the glass at all the fruits and granola she had yet to either toss or store.

Ivy looked up and smiled with a wiggle of her fingertips in greeting. "Fawn, I hope we won't be much trouble so close to closing time. Charlie begged me for one of your smoothies."

Fawn laughed and shook her head. "I'd be honored to make Mr. Charlie whatever he wants." She winked at Ivy. "And whatever you allow."

Charlie's eyes lit up. He flashed Ivy a white-tooth smile. "Can I get the Cocoa Wonder, Mom? Please?"

Ivy chewed her lower lip, contemplating her answer, although the glimmer in her eyes told Fawn she wouldn't deny her son what he wanted. Ivy Merrow, werewolf from a rival pack in South Carolina, came to Nocturne Falls by way of a prearranged marriage agreement to Hank Merrow. It hadn't been all stardust and fairy lights in the beginning, but the two made a beautiful couple. Hank had fallen into the father role seamlessly, and Charlie thrived as a werewolf and a brother to little sister, Hannah Rose.

But he still had his mother wrapped around his finger.

"Oh, why not. Fawn, is that okay?" Ivy asked.

Fawn smiled—her first genuine smile since she noticed Kalen at the table—and started filling a metal cup with ingredients.

"Now, Charlie, how much cocoa you want?" She took the lid off the cocoa powder in the buffet, tapped a finger to the plastic third pan, and arced her hand to the metal cup. A stream of cocoa followed, flowing magically into the cup. "Tell me when to stop."

Fawn waited a few moments for the boy to tell her to stop, but his instruction never came. Instead, his smile grew and his eyes glowed with excitement as he watched her small performance of magic.

"Charlie," Ivy said sternly.

"Okay, that's enough." His shoulders slumped. "Thanks, Miss Fawn. Mom, I'm going to use the bathroom."

"You and Charlie having a mother-son date night, I see. Hank's home with Hannah Rose?" Fawn asked, watching Charlie hurry down the narrow hallway to the public bathroom.

"Yeah. It's been a few weeks since we've had some time, just Charlie and me," Ivy said. Before Fawn could turn away, Ivy caught her eyes and her smile faded. "Hank filled me in on the accident by your place the other night. Pretty wild, huh?"

Fawn shrugged. "Alex stopped by shortly after it happened, I guess. I hadn't heard anything, and I didn't have any information for him."

Ivy leaned a little closer to the glass display. "Well, consider yourself lucky you didn't come into contact with anyone. That accident smelled suspicious from the moment he was called to it. There was no sign of injury, no documentation, no evidence of someone leaving the car, no fingerprints. Nothing. When he ran the plate, it came back to someone from Wyoming. When he called, the suspected owner was unknown. He's tracing the car using the VIN and hoping to catch a break, but he thinks it was stolen and we've got some crazy fugitive running free."

Fawn almost dropped the metal cup, but managed to tighten her fingers before the thing slipped out of her grip. A faint tremor touched her hands and she turned away, hoping Ivy didn't pick up on her sudden shift into discomfort. As she poured the ingredients into a blender, she contemplated whether agreeing to speak with Kalen in private was the smartest thing to do.

"Well, I'll be locking my doors at night," Fawn assured, flipping the switch on the blender. The loud drone of the blade liquefying the ingredients proved enough cover for the shred of unease unraveled by the conversation. The sobering reminder that she knew nothing about this strange creature she had agreed to speak with left her shifting uncomfortably on her feet.

Maybe she should tell Ivy the suspect was going to be in the parking lot in forty-five minutes.

No. He needs your help. He's trusting you.

Damn conscience. She couldn't forget the raw desperation she sensed in him, as hard as she tried. The man was in serious need of...something.

She touched her forehead where his lips had brushed a tender kiss. Spirits, she was mad to be going out with a stranger and not telling anyone.

Charlie returned by the time she flipped the blender off and poured the drink into a cup. She regained a dose of her old smile and ramped up the wattage as she handed the smoothie to the boy.

Ivy pulled out her wallet, but Fawn waved it aside. "On me. It's always nice to see you two. And thanks for the update."

Ivy plunked a ten-dollar bill in the tip jar, shooting Fawn a warning glance when she began to protest.

"For another plant to add to your garden. Don't try to give it back and don't threaten to tell Hank."

Fawn rolled her eyes, but smiled. She dropped to her forearms on the check-out counter and folded her hands. "It worked the time you thought I'd missed the twenty you left."

Ivy's manicured brows lifted. "No, it didn't, because you still had the twenty when Hank did nothing more than grumble under his breath."

She draped an arm around Charlie's narrow shoulders. He possessed a thinner build than most werewolves at ten, but he was a damn handsome boy.

"Catch you around, Fawn. And thanks again."

"Thanks, Miss Fawn," Charlie added, sipping his smoothie.

"Anytime, you two. Careful out there. Weather isn't going to hold out much longer."

Even inside her shop, her body could sense the impending storm. The weight of the wind and rain pressed down on her shoulders, ghostly pressure stirring her wild nature.

She waited for Ivy and Charlie to walk past the last window at the front of the shop before she rounded the counter and locked the door.

Nine-thirty sped up on her heels before she knew it. As she turned off the lights, secured her safe in the office, and gathered her bag and keys, she tried to make sense of the fluttering in her chest and the churn of her stomach. A strange prickle traced the area his lips had touched against her forehead and the finger he had healed.

In all of her twenty-seven years, she had never, ever felt this strong connection with a man. Fates must've found it entertaining that he happened to be an out-of-town stranger with secrets when she was by nature forthcoming and honest. Except when it came to answering a deputy's questions about a captivating supernatural.

Oh, but he's worthy eye candy.

That was for sure.

Fawn slipped out the back door and into the humid night. A single light glowed dimly over the stoop, enough to highlight her exact position while the pitch of night doused the rest of the lot. She had mentioned the lack of lighting to the landlord a handful of times, but nothing had been done to rectify the problem. She turned toward the lot, her back to the locked door, and scanned the area for Kalen. No one. She glanced at her watch and saw she was late. Well, if he couldn't forgive her five minutes, then he didn't need to talk to her that badly after all.

Yet, with every foot she stepped closer to her car, more tension swelled across her shoulders and back. She would not entertain the idea it wasn't necessarily a *bad* tension.

When she pulled open her door and began to slide behind the wheel, she realized why.

Half of her body in the car, the other half holding her weight balanced in a precarious position, she stared at Kalen, seated like a bunched-up hoodlum in her passenger seat. The hood of his jacket hung over his head and shadowed his face, along with the sunglasses.

"It's nighttime," she stated the obvious, slowly lowering to her seat. "Do you really need those to cover your eyes?"

"You've seen my eyes. What is your explanation of the color?"

Oh, the arrogance. How she could do without it.

"Are you going to continue to be a jerk?" she asked tersely. Kalen's head twisted, the movement vaguely noticeable beneath the hood.

"I don't understand."

"A jerk. Rude. Condescending. Aggravating." She kept one foot flat on the ground outside her car, one hand leashed on the side of the door. Just in case she needed leverage to escape, whether from a threat or frustration. Kalen's head tilted. "No power trip. If you want help or a listening ear, the attitude goes. Now."

"I was unaware I had an...attitude."

The genuine bafflement in his voice struck a cord inside her. She tried to stay mad and on guard, but something about his demeanor was...off.

The corners of his mouth tugged downward. His gaze shifted from her to stare out the passenger window.

"I apologize."

Oh-kay.

There was definitely an ocean's depth of *more* to this creature than she initially thought.

"Apology accepted." Fawn pulled her foot into the car and closed the door. "How did you know this was my car?"

"I saw it at your house." He lifted a hand, long fingers splayed, and swiped it above the dashboard. "You resonate within its structure. Your energy is powerful. It's...soothing."

Another layer of resolve shredded away from her. The defensive edge in his voice had completely drained away to reveal a twinge of vulnerability.

"I noticed the night of the accident, but I hadn't seen the reason why."

At last, he pushed the hood back from his head, revealing his ash-blond hair. He had it pulled half back, with only a few shorter strands escaping to brush over his brows. His ears, blunt like a hybrid human-fairy, were exposed. The shade of pale to his skin conflicted with the skin tone of the fae she knew. Willa Iscove, fae friend and magical jeweler extraordinaire, sported a decent tan during the summer months. Kalen's skin was the kind of pale that said he spent little, if any, time soaking in the sun.

Kalen lowered his sunglasses from his face, folding the arms in a deliberate motion.

"You're elven. Nature," he said, his voice almost a whisper.

Fawn nodded. "I am. A descendant of the Brandonian race."

Kalen finally turned his stunning eyes on her and the air turned dense and hard to breathe. She fumbled with her keys, turning away to get her bearings, and shoved the key into the ignition.

"I make you nervous." The sadness in his voice made her pause and dare another glance at him. "I don't want you to be nervous with me. I know that feeling, and I would never wish it upon anyone."

"I'm not nervous," she protested, twisting the key. The engine hitched and rolled, coming to life with a purr. "I'm trying to figure you out. I mean, you crack up your expensive car, leave my house when the deputy shows up—"

"Let us go to Jackson's house. I need to check on my sister."

Talk about shutting down a conversation.

"Want to start by sharing why you're hiding?" Fawn asked, tossing the bait in hopes she wasn't too off track with her speculation. A subtle chilling sensation touched her skin, one that swiftly followed Kalen straightening up in the passenger seat. Mustn't be too far off.

"What makes you believe I'm hiding?"

"Very few people crack up a Beamer and avoid law enforcement like the plague all in the same night." Fawn backed out of the spot, her gaze brushing Kalen as she settled back in her seat and popped the shifter into Drive. She left out the part about no fingerprints or forensic evidence, and the call to Wyoming. Until she knew more about the hot mystery man beside her, she wasn't sharing her own information. She drove out of the parking lot and away from Main Street, toward the residential area of Nocturne Falls. "Sheriff Merrow suspects the car is stolen."

"It wasn't stolen."

"Then why won't you speak with the authorities?"

"There are reasons."

"Care to share those reasons?"

"No." Kalen placed his sunglasses back on his nose and turned to the passenger window again. "Not at this time."

"You're not very good at conversation," she mumbled.

"No. I'm not."

Quirking a brow and slowing the car in the middle of the street, she looked at him. "Your hearing is quite exceptional for a…fairy?"

"Only part fae."

"And?"

"No."

His short answer assured her she wasn't going to get anywhere trying to discover his full heritage, at least for now. "Who is this Jackson fellow?"

"Jackson Emery. A friend."

Ah, Jackson. She knew Jackson Emery from his weekly visit to her shop for a Naturalistic Delicious granola bowl. "Where does he live?"

Kalen sighed. "Should I drive?"

Fawn's eyes went wide. She stared at him, incredulous, for a long moment before she laughed. Kalen's forehead creased and his lips turned down once more.

"Why do you laugh?"

"You want me to trust you with my car?" She shook her head and pressed on the accelerator again. "I had a front-row seat to your driving skills, if you've forgotten. I'm not impressed."

"That was an accident."

"Touché."

"I don't understand."

"How about we go back to my place and talk there?"

Kalen shook his head. "No. I need to check on my sister."

"What's wrong with her? Is she in trouble? Is that why you won't tell me anything? Or talk to the police? Is that why you ran from the accident and my home when I was trying to help you?"

She wanted answers, needed answers, because the mental storm that rolled off him in monstrous waves and crashed down onto her shoulders was taking its toll. If she had been alone, she might have banged her head against the steering wheel a time or two. Or a dozen. She didn't even know this guy, yet she felt deep down, be it the death of her, she could not walk away from the tumultuous creature. Damn the Fates for throwing him at her.

Or, maybe that's *why* he crashed into her life.

Literally.

As she drove toward the hills and mountains of Nocturne Falls where the residential communities resided, silence stretched. Minutes ticked away as the quiet inside the car filled with tension.

Kalen dropped a hand over hers, which rested high on her thigh. The intimacy of the touch startled her. She stiffened, half wanting to throw his hand off, half wanting to see what he was going to do. She began to wonder whether this guy had any idea of what propriety was, or if it remained one of the elusive things he *didn't know.*

"I asked to return to Jackson for my sister, yes. But also because I'm not familiar with…"

Kalen cleared his throat. The faint twitch of his fingers over hers caught her attention. Their touch, as it had earlier and on the night of the accident, elicited more primal emotions inside her than she cared to acknowledge. But, had she not, she would have missed this teeny hint to his lack of confidence.

"I am not good around people and I don't want to offend you more than I have."

His touch provided a reassurance of safety, despite the conflicting sense that he was far from safe. Fawn moistened her lips, shocked to find them so dry, and nodded.

"Okay. To Jackson's place it is. I warn you, don't try to pull anything. I know how to defend myself."

The corner of Kalen's mouth twitched, and for a brief moment, she could have sworn he almost grinned. He moved his hand away to rest it on his knee, leaving her with a sudden emptiness in her gut.

She followed his fluid directions to a small cottage at the end of a street. Half the yard was flanked by trees, the other half questionably landscaped before a fence closed off the property from a neighbor's. A dented-up Civic sat in the driveway. A single dull yellow light bulb cast the front stoop in a sickly glow. Fawn pulled up to the curb and cut the engine, chewing at her lower lip.

"This is the place?" she asked, wondering about her decision to agree to this.

Kalen climbed out of the car with the grace and fluidity of a ghost in fae skin. He moved as if the air became one with him. Fawn stared at his back after he closed the door and started up the driveway.

Perhaps she should take the opportunity to bolt.

Kalen paused, raising his hand to the back of his neck. He cast a glance over his shoulder. That worried crease in his forehead was back, and becoming awfully familiar.

One moment, Fawn felt the power of his gaze through those silly sunglasses. The next, her door was pulled open and he was there.

She let out a small shriek.

Kalen stretched out a hand. "I didn't mean to frighten you."

Her heart threatened to pound its way out of her chest. "You are a conundrum, aren't you." She didn't want to take his hand. Really, really didn't want to take his hand.

She dropped her hand in his and allowed him to help her from the car.

"A what?"

Fawn waved the question aside, closing her door and locking up. Nocturne Falls didn't have "bad" areas, per se, but that didn't mean she had to trust this particular house or street.

She also didn't necessarily trust the guy who continued to hold her hand as he led the way up the drive.

So strange.

That she allowed the physical contact to continue was even more worrisome. She didn't understand the pull. Yes, he was breathtakingly gorgeous, but thus far, nothing else should have made him attractive. His attitude sure sucked and he didn't talk much.

If she wanted a relationship with a statue, she'd have one commissioned. One that smiled.

So why couldn't she kick the connection between them? What was it about Kalen that made her want to stay? To understand? To walk to the creepy house with a stranger and a woman who'd tried to gouge out her throat a few nights ago?

What world had she crossed into?

She slowed her step as they approached the door.

She stopped completely when Kalen flicked his hand and the door opened. On its own.

"Wait a minute." Fawn twisted her hand out of his gentle grip and stepped back, shaking her head. She felt absolutely no hint of energy through his skin for that little magic trick. She shot her gaze up to Kalen. "What race of fae are you part of?"

Kalen shrugged. "I don't know."

Fawn took another step back. "What do you mean?"

"Exactly that. I don't know what fae race runs in my blood. I was never told."

Oh, that tornado was barreling toward her, prepared to take her way past Oz.

Kalen lifted his sunglasses onto his head and her heart damn near sputtered to a stop when she saw the raw despair that filled those swirling crystals of color.

"I know many things, and yet, I know so little."

The shields Fawn had put in place against this man-creature crumbled. She tilted her head, gauging him more closely, trying to understand him, read him, feel something from his aura and his spirit that would make sense to her.

"I want to make one thing clear, Kalen Hawkins. I'm not the type of woman who allows a man to lick her finger without knowing his name first. And since I went against that personal rule, I want to know what makes up the fang-and-healing part of you."

A new voice interrupted them. "Oh, that's easy." A ruffled Jackson appeared in the doorway, pushing wire-rimmed glasses up the bridge of his nose. "That's the vampire part."

Chapter 5

"I wish I could tell you a lie and somehow make it a truth, Kalen. I wish I could paint you a picture with bright colors and promise, but there will always be darkness. Always shadows. Doubt. Danger. And the promise of no promises. You will always look over your shoulder and always proceed with caution. To do so, you can't tell people, even those you think you can trust, what you are. You must hide one or the other factor of your breed. Never show both. Unless, should the gods bless you after the horror you've endured, you find someone who calls to a place so deep inside your soul that you can only reach it with that person's help, loneliness will be your companion. Loneliness will be your safety."

"You brought her back," Vivian whispered in her partially sedated state, pulling Kalen from his thoughts of Nicholas. He nodded, brushing the hair from her closed eyes. A weak smile curved her mouth. "I knew you would."

"Jackson said she could be trusted. She's elven."

"Your breeding does not make you trustworthy, Kalen," she reminded him. "Your heart does."

He sighed and nodded. "You must've watched more of those romantic movies Nicholas brought us than I. You speak with a lover's tongue. So poetic, little sister."

"And you, my brother?" Her small hand reached to rest on his knee. "You carry a burden on your shoulders that has defined you, created you, and will destroy you, if you allow it."

"Nicholas once said that which creates us, destroys us. I find more truth in that statement every day."

"Well, now. Don't be so drab." Vivian pulled her hand away and rolled to her side, giving her back to Kalen. "Go back to the woman and Jackson."

Kalen sat for a few more minutes, watching Vivian's small form curl up beneath the blanket. He waited until her breaths evened and her mind became restful. Only then could he bring himself to leave her side for the woman in the kitchen.

An elf who stirred magic inside his body and refused to release him from her image. That magic intensified when she was near. In the three days since the accident, she had turned into his secret…fantasy.

Jackson tried to keep him in the house, but he had spent his life locked up in a room. He'd tasted freedom, devoured it, craved it, wanted more. He hadn't expected Nicholas's nephew to have the wit to follow him into the main part of this strange paranormal town.

Two days into his explosive arrival, he wandered to the streets of Nocturne Falls, wide-eyed, mouth agape, drinking in the magnificence and splendor of the festive town. Hidden beneath a jacket, hat, plain clothing, and dark sunglasses, he practically drowned in the battering stimulation of colors, crowds, and chaos. The succulent aromas that wafted from places called "pubs" and "restaurants" made his mouth water and his stomach grumble. The strangely alluring bitterness of another shop—he duly noted Hallowed Bean as the name—piqued his curiosity. He tucked the place away to explore at a later date.

He recognized several other supernatural creatures by their peculiar energies, wolves and cats and bears. Others he didn't. He heard the almost silent crackle of rock from a statue at the fountain. Humans muttered and gasped the word "gargoyle". Another piece of information he'd look up once he returned the Jackson's house. All of these other creatures, like himself, wove seamlessly through throngs of humans in a peaceful waltz.

As he walked aimlessly back to the hustle of Main Street—he couldn't control his delight enough to stay in one place long—he sensed the curiosity of another vampire.

It was then that Jackson caught up with him and dragged him into the closest store, a stored filled with food items that smelled immensely sweet and delicious to the point Kalen's jaw tightened and he helped himself to a bag of something called pralines.

He learned two things in that store. One, he couldn't take the "merchandise" without paying for it first. Second, the owner, Delaney Ellingham, was a vampire as well. A very inquisitive vampire who questioned him about who he was, what he was, and had him fleeing the store before she started to unravel his identity.

A vampire. Awake and walking in daylight.

He was not alone in this inverted warp town, and for the first time in his life, he felt…comfortable.

Kalen reached the kitchen, but paused at the archway. He leaned against the wall, his attention drawn to the woman seated beside Jackson, angled close to the computer screen as Nicholas's nephew rambled on and on about the data on a spreadsheet. Residual sweetness touched his nostrils as the essence of fruit and natural sweets clung to Faunalyn from a day spent working in her shop.

He had happened by Faunalyn's shop the first day he ventured into town. A place called Magical Mayhem, Smoothies and More. He stood outside, watching her from the sidewalk, unable to explain his enamored head. The night of the accident, her hair had been in a messy style, hiding her ears. He had been too anxious to dissect her beyond the fact she was beautiful and sparked a light that had been dead inside him. But that afternoon, lost in watching her move with ease, that bright, promising smile and those warm, caring eyes, all he could think about was how to make her smile like that for him.

It struck him at that moment. The dire complexity of Faunalyn.

He wanted to *feel*. He didn't understand it, but he needed Faunalyn to know him, accept him.

He wanted to understand why his body ached and his mind spun and his sluggish heart sped at the very thought of her. He wanted to understand the heat that swelled inside him and the light that ignited and the desire to be with her and never again alone.

"Her name is Faunalyn Ayres. She's beautiful, isn't she?" Jackson had asked from behind him as Kalen stared. *"There are many people in this town whom you can befriend. But, Fawn? Fawn you can trust. Her heart is as pure as untouched nature. She thrives on bringing peace and happiness to those who are her friends. She has an impeccable reputation in this town for helping others."*

Trust. That damning and deceptive word. Trust.

Gods, to *trust* someone again. Aside from Vivian, the only other people he trusted were Nicholas and Jackson, the latter only through Nicholas's assurance.

"I was beginning to worry about you," Jackson said, looking up from his laptop. Faunalyn twisted in her chair to look at him. Kalen tamped down the dark tentacle that licked along his mind at the sight of the two hunched close to one another. "I had started to explain a little about you and Vivian to Fawn. You know, to help her understand why you're supposed to remain elusive." He cleared his throat rather deliberately, his brows arching. "Why you aren't supposed to go gallivanting around town."

"You can walk in the sunlight. There are only a few vampires who can do that, and their secrets are closely guarded."

Fawn's statement was filled with wonder. Kalen swallowed down the foul feelings spurred by Jackson's nearness to Faunalyn and crossed to the table. The entire time, her gaze swept over him, creating crackling paths of heat every place she looked. He'd have to investigate the cause of that. Determine if she was placing some kind of elven spell on him.

He pulled a chair up to Faunalyn's empty side and sat down. His leg rested against hers, setting something fierce in motion inside him. His body thrummed and ached, and a subtle tremor shot through his fingers.

"I have to ask, so don't take offense," she said. Why did her gaze linger on his mouth? Why did her cheeks turn pink when she met his eyes? He knew what it meant when her pupils swelled, though. "Do you have a heartbeat?"

Kalen opened his hand, palm up. "Allow me your hand."

Faunalyn took her time placing her hand in his. He turned her hand over as he lifted it and pressed her palm to his chest. Again, small shocks swept through his skin, even though his T-shirt acted as a barrier between them.

He adored the way her eyes widened and her lips parted on a soft gasp. "Sweet goddess, you do. Very slow, but it's there. How is this possible? How are *you* possible?"

"He and Vivian were the product of a twisted scientist looking for a way to live forever without being forced into darkness," Jackson said. Kalen peeled his gaze from Faunalyn and looked over her golden head to take in Jackson's disheveled appearance. He wondered if the kid realized his hair was always a mess and his clothes were from yesterday.

"For one who stands strong behind surreptitiousness, you are quite outspoken about my situation," Kalen pointed out sternly.

Jackson's face turned red. He rubbed his cheeks, but straightened his shoulders in defiance. "Listen. I might be a microbiologist with more knowledge about your situation than anyone else in this area, but I'm one person. Since you came without my uncle, I'm a little unprepared. All I have to go on is the information he sent me over the last few years in preparation for your arrival, and the funds he'd set up for me to take on this task. You need someone you can trust and who might be willing to help while keeping your existence under wraps. Fawn can be trusted. Besides, you're obviously smitten with her."

Confusion settled in his mind. He narrowed his gaze on Jackson, who had returned to the dizzying displays on his computer.

"Care to embellish on what 'smitten' is?"

Jackson laughed, hitching his finger at Kalen. "This guy. He knows how to use 'surreptitiousness' but has no idea what 'smitten' is."

Kalen hadn't realized he still held Faunalyn's hand until her fingers wiggled in his grip. He reluctantly released her. That hand found his knee and gave him a gentle pat. Her smile soothed him, melting away the frustration.

"Don't worry about it. I don't think it's a correct observation anyhow." Her delicate brow creased. "How's your sister?"

"Resting."

"So..." Faunalyn shifted, turning back to the computer screen. "Jackson was showing me notes from a file about some tests. I'm no microbiologist like Mr. Genius here, but it looked like blood work and a genetic screening. You said your sister's ill."

Kalen's mouth twitched. His attention flicked between Jackson and Faunalyn. How much did she know? How much had she figured out? What had Jackson told her?

"Yes." Kalen focused on the notes that popped up on the screen. Notes from Dr. Hamstead about Vivian's transition. He didn't know what the madman was trying to do, but whatever it was, it was ripping his beloved sister apart from the inside. "We're here to try and figure out the cure. Nicholas believed his nephew could help."

Faunalyn's questioning gaze ran deep. "Who's Nicholas and his nephew?"

Jackson raised his hand. "Nephew here."

"Nicholas was a...friend," Kalen said. The word hung on his tongue, right and steadfast. The truth behind his statement delivered a sickening punch to his conscience.

"What happened?"

"He died," Jackson said, cutting the answer in quickly before Kalen could fumble with his words. He'd told Jackson about his uncle's demise. He didn't care to share those details with Faunalyn. Not yet. "I get to play host to Mr. Moody and his lovely sister—when she's not trying to snap my head off—and figure out a cure to this mess."

"And where do I come in?" Faunalyn asked.

"I told you, he's smitten." Jackson shrugged. "And I know you can be trusted. He needs to be assimilated into everyday life. He and his sister have been caged up for most of their lives."

The shock that struck Faunalyn's features as she jerked around and stared at him sent a bout of unease through his body.

"Are you serious?"

"Jackson, must we discuss this?" Kalen asked.

"Do you want her to understand why you act like a Neanderthal half the time?" Jackson's fingers ran mad over the keyboard. "Because it would make life much less complicated. Now, I gave Vivian a bit more of the sedative tonight so I can work through this genetic screw-up by the good doctor and hopefully come up with something sooner than later that won't require Alice Bishop's assistance. That won't go over well, especially since she's employed by Eleanora Ellingham. I hate politics of all types, and I'd much rather keep this away from the queen of Nocturne Falls. So, I don't need you scowling down my neck, Kalen."

"You're impossible," Kalen groused, fighting the urge to flash his fangs.

"Hey, I have an idea." Faunalyn abruptly stood and smiled. "I haven't had dinner yet, and it's late. Why don't we go into town, grab some take-out and go back to my place? That way, Jackson can work and you can fill me in on things."

Kalen shouldn't have felt the relief he did, but something about Faunalyn sang to a deep section of his soul.

"If anything happens to Vivian—"

"*Nothing* will happen to her." Jackson pushed his glasses up and shot him a glower. Kalen might not understand emotions like most, but he caught the blame in that single look. "Go. You're in good hands with Fawn."

Kalen couldn't help but wonder about that statement. Jackson said it casually, but the sentiment resonated with fire in his belly. The light blush that highlighted Faunalyn's cheeks made him wonder if she felt something similar.

"You're willing to spend time with a... Neanderthal?" Kalen asked.

That smile again, warm and contagious. Faunalyn snatched up his hands and tugged his arms. "Come on. Let me introduce you to some Nocturne Falls grub."

Chapter 6

"Why does that place always smell like it's burning?" Kalen asked. Fawn glanced out his window. Lips taut, he pointed to the Hallowed Bean. The coffee shop's customers were dwindling as the night pressed on. Almost eleven o'clock, and many of the food and beverage stores were getting ready to close. "It's strange. I can't decide if I like the smell or not."

"Hallowed Bean is *the* staple coffee houses in Nocturne Falls."

Kalen twisted enough to look at her, a deft mixture of curiosity and confusion rolling around his expression. "Coffee?"

Fawn nodded. "Yeah. They sell all sorts of wonderful coffee and tea beverages, as well as some pretty delicious bakery items."

"What exactly is coffee?"

Fawn jammed on her brakes and gaped at Kalen. He put a hand on the dash as the car jerked to a stop.

There was not a speck of humor in his eyes. The guy was dead serious.

"You've never heard of coffee?"

He shook his head. "I've seen it in movies, but always wondered what it was."

She felt her eyes widen. "Movies?"

Kalen remained silent. After a few moments, his expression shuttered and he turned back to the window. "Never mind."

"Oh, no, no, no." Fawn cut the steering wheel to the right and guided her car into the closest open parking spot. She cut the engine and removed the keys. "Come on."

"Where?"

"I'm officially introducing you to the mortal equivalent of ambrosia."

Fawn waited for Kalen on the sidewalk as he took his sweet time climbing out of her car and stepping up to her side. He wore his sunglasses again despite the darkness, and Fawn had to force herself not to giggle. At least he would get away with his eccentricity in this town.

As she led him into the coffee shop, she wondered about the truth in Jackson's statement regarding the siblings. She hadn't believed he was literal when he said they spent most of their lives locked up, but the longer she was with Kalen, the more she realized he was oblivious to everyday things. Things most people, herself included, took for granted.

He stood awfully close to her side. As if unconsciously, his fingers brushed the back of her hand as he looked up at the menu board.

"What am I reading?" he asked quietly.

Fawn frowned. She pressed up on her toes and whispered in his ear, "Can you read?"

His head jerked away and the intensity of his gaze from behind the sunglasses was sweltering. "Of *course* I can read."

"Sorry," she muttered, taking a half-step back. She hadn't wanted to offend him. She didn't know what she was dealing with. "I didn't mean it to come out that way."

To her surprise, Kalen shifted, swallowing up the small distance between them. When his fingers brushed hers this time, they curled around her hand.

"I'm well-educated, Faunalyn. That doesn't mean I'm versed in society." He motioned to the menu board with a wave of his hand. "I have no idea what any of those things are." He glanced down at her. "Why don't you choose something you think I might like?"

"Give me something to work with. Do you like sweet? Bold? Bitter? Rich flavors? Subtle flavors?"

"I enjoyed your tea."

Fawn's eyes narrowed. His frequent changes of topic could give her whiplash.

"Would you prefer tea?"

His fingers tightened. "How about I *trust* you to make the decision for me? I'd very much like to try this *coffee*."

Fawn smiled and nodded, giving his hand a squeeze back. The gesture came unnervingly naturally, like holding his hand. "Okay. But you're not allowed to get mad at me if you don't like it, since I have no idea what I'm working with."

"Sweet," he said. "But not too sweet."

Fawn ordered two caramel lattes and a triple berry scone she saw him eyeing. Drinks and pastry in hand, Fawn led him back to the car. Seated inside, he sniffed the drink before taking a cautious sip.

A long, tenuous moment slipped by. He took another sip.

Fawn raised a brow. "So?"

Kalen sipped again, then again. He licked his top lip, lifted the cup level with his eyes, and scrutinized it. "Delicious." He lowered the cup and pinned her with a sincere glance. "But not as delicious as your tea."

Fawn laughed. She tapped her cup to his in salute and nodded. "I'll drink to that. First coffee: success."

As she drove toward Howler's Bar and Grill to pick up take-out, she was acutely aware of Kalen's gaze on her every few moments. She smiled inside over his small sips of coffee, absorbing his child-like curiosity and hidden excitement. The town's streets glowed with fairy lights, adding to the magical feel of the costumed tourists. Nighttime performers—usually paranormal residents playing their true selves for the entertainment of the tourists—were packing up for the night.

"Why didn't you tell the police officer about me after the crash?" Kalen's question caught her completely off guard.

Flustered, she struggled for an explanation that didn't sound ridiculous. "Something told me not to."

Pretty ridiculous, Fawn.

"You had no reason to protect me or my sister." He touched a single finger to the back of her hand. She had to bite back the urge to acknowledge those strange sparks. Again. "You did something to her. When she attacked you, you were able to calm her. How did you do it?"

Fawn's memories rolled back to that night. To that moment when she reached for the car door to open it and make sure everyone was okay and found herself under attack. In those crucial moments of shock and fear, she did the only thing she knew to do.

"I called on the Earth for Her power."

"You can use the Earth for power?"

"Can't you?"

She glanced at him as he slowly shook his head.

"I was never taught, so I'm not sure. The small things I can do with magic I've learned by accident or instinct."

Her heart cracked a little at this revelation. Being of fae blood and not understanding one's own magical ability was almost as unheard of as vampires never having a thirst for blood. It just didn't happen. She was elven, but elves and fae were distant cousins. They shared many of the same power sources. Her strongest sources were those directly linked to Mother Earth.

"Kalen." She wasn't certain how to proceed without him closing her out. Any attempt to get more information seemed to shut him down. Tentatively, she said, "Jackson said you had a sheltered life. How sheltered?"

"Jackson didn't say 'sheltered.' I'm afraid if we were 'sheltered,' we'd be far better off. What he said was we were caged." The sullen air that rippled around him drenched the car with a somber resonance. He lowered his sunglasses to his lap with a quiet sigh.

She couldn't believe it. "Caged? As in metal bars?"

"As in being locked in a room except for when we were brought into a lab for testing."

The data spreadsheets from Jackson's files came to mind. Her stomach flipped in a sickening way. An ache grew in her chest. "What were you being tested for?"

Kalen shrugged. "Many things."

Fawn fought for words, but nothing came. There was nothing to say, nothing she *could* say to this despicable bit of news. She knew it wasn't impossible. Now, when she looked at Kalen, the reflection of his eyes in the window revealed his eagerness to take every little detail in without missing a moment, and that crack in her heart shattered. What she lived every day for twenty-seven years, he was only now experiencing.

"How old are you?" Like she needed another hammer hit to her sympathetic overload.

"Thirty-one. My understanding is Vivian and I are children compared to others of our species, both of them." He tore his attention from the window long enough to survey her. "Right?"

"Well, the vampires I know are a few hundred years old, except for Delaney, who's much younger. The fae I know range in age."

"You're younger than I." He frowned. "At least, I think you are. Aren't elves related to fae?"

Fawn nodded once. "I'm 27. And yes. Elves are distantly related to the fae." Kalen's reserved attitude and his uncanny gestures and reactions were starting to make sense. Understanding didn't lighten the mood in the least, so she picked up the paper bag with the scone and handed it to Kalen. "Here. You were practically drooling over it at Hallowed Bean."

"You were watching?"

She flashed him a smile. "It's kinda hard to ignore a grown man leaving nose prints on the glass of the display case."

He took the bag. "I was *not*."

"I beg to differ. We can turn around and I can show you the dot art." She pulled into the back lot of Howler's and cut the engine. When she looked at Kalen, the air whooshed from her lungs. "And...you smile."

Only, there was more to his smile than a simple show of perfect teeth and curled lips. His smile was stunning, as much as he was. It made his eyes glitter and washed away the sadness.

Kalen broke a piece off the corner of the scone. He brought it to his nose, seemingly unaware of Fawn's jump in body temperature. "Smells great."

"Do you want…to come in?" Fawn asked, clearing her throat against the husk.

"I'd prefer to indulge in this. The sunglasses would be silly inside, would they not?"

Damn him for that shadowed side-glance as he popped the scone into his mouth. She gathered it was his attempt at a joke.

"Yes, they would. And Bridget would probably question you about them. So, enjoy and don't wander about alone."

The moment she stepped out of the car and closed the door, air filled her lungs again. She hadn't realized how difficult it had become to simply be around Kalen. His past was obviously dismal and dark, and the weight of his secrets hung like spikes waiting to plunge into her spirit.

Without understanding how, she knew it was only a matter of time before her happy little world took a turn for disaster.

Coffee.

Now he understood the allure. It was strange—both bitter and sweet—but something about the flavor, how it burst along his tongue and filled his senses with delight, instantly won him.

It was nothing compared to the companionship of the woman beside him.

Kalen chewed at small pieces of the scone, the buttery sweetness sending him into another dimension. Oh, the things he'd missed all his life. Simple things, he gathered, that he'd never known or tasted or felt. Like the dull shockwaves that skittered along his skin every time he touched Faunalyn. He wondered if it was her magic, or something else. He'd seen many other women since escaping the lab, but not a single one did to his senses what the pretty elf accomplished.

He put the remaining scone in the bag and folded the top to bring to Vivi. His sister would thoroughly enjoy the treat.

Kalen sat in the car, still as stone, waiting for Faunalyn to return. He mentally counted the minutes—a familiar pastime when he was bored in his prison. He became anxious as the fifteen-minute mark rolled around. The car grew stuffy. He twisted in the seat, gauging the uninhabited surroundings, and decided it was fine to get some fresh air.

As soon as he opened the door, the aromatic air hit him hard, sending his stomach into a grumbling fit. He'd barely eaten since the escape, and his body finally forced him to acknowledge his hunger. The thumping music from within the building mixed with raucous laughter and loud talk. His ears ached from the noise. The lab had always been quiet, with moderate noise levels. The world outside those cursed walls continued to shock his sensitive senses, reminding him he had yet to learn who he truly was, and whether he could control parts of himself.

Despite the assault on his ears, Kalen headed to the building Faunalyn disappeared into. The door swung open easily. For a long moment, he stood in the doorway, observing the crowd. Green-topped tables sat in a line, a mixture of humans and paranormals hitting colored balls with long sticks into holes. Across the way, circular plaques hung on walls dotted by short sticks with colored plastic feathers. He tilted his head and narrowed his eyes.

Peculiar.

"'Xuse us."

Kalen stepped aside to allow three young women to sidle by. One's gaze lingered on him, a wicked smile curving her red-painted lips. Kalen resumed his search for Faunalyn. He didn't understand the unease that touched his gut at the woman's smile, but it urged him to hurry to the elf's side. Not a danger, but a self-conscious recognition that he wanted to be near Faunalyn.

Incredibly strange, these feelings.

He listened to the different voices and subtly sniffed the different scents until he honed in on the one he sought. Following the sugar-laced smell of smoothie shop and coffee, he spotted the elf standing at a long bar, talking to a woman and a man. The woman was pretty, with golden eyes and wild hair. The man was serious and large, a force to be reckoned with. Kalen smelled the animal in them both, but couldn't place their particular species.

Faunalyn's gaze slid to Kalen. Her smile grew and her eyes lit up, those soft lavender hues weakening him at the knees. She motioned for him to join her. The man's blue eyes followed him to Faunalyn's side, the assessing look in them reminding Kalen of a couple of doctors at the lab after they injected him with one thing or another. The scrutiny ignited both his fury and sense of vulnerability.

Kalen didn't like this man.

The woman, on the other hand, offered him a wave. "Can I getchya a drink?"

Kalen glanced at Faunalyn. Her brows arched. "Do you want something? A soda? A water? A beer?"

His brows furrowed. When he opened his mouth to ask, she laughed and waved him silent. The motion, he realized, saved him from a huge falter—asking why he would want a drink when he'd entered an establishment the primary purpose of which was to serve them.

"A water will be fine. Thank you," Kalen finally said.

"Kalen, this is Hank Merrow, Nocturne Falls' sheriff. And Bridget, his sister, is getting your water. She owns Howler's," Faunalyn introduced.

Kalen eyed the man more closely. "Sheriff." He held out a hand, following the seemingly mundane protocol upon introductions. "Nice to meet you."

Merrow glanced at his hand before accepting the gesture with a firm grip. "Same. I didn't catch your name."

"Kalen."

Hank nodded once, but his gaze remained hard. "You visiting Fawn?"

"Yes," Faunalyn interjected smoothly, placing a hand on Kalen's before he could answer. He was beginning to think silence was his best route. Judging by Hank's probing gaze, he'd be best to trust Faunalyn to lead him through this obstacle.

Perhaps he should have stayed in the car.

Bridget returned with a glass of water. Kalen thanked her. There wasn't much trouble he could get into with a simple thanks, he hoped.

"How're you liking the town so far?" Bridget asked. Kalen took a sip from the glass.

"Nice," he said, following Nicholas's advice.

Keep things short. Answer the question, and only the question with as few words as possible. Never leave yourself open for speculation.

"How long are you planning to stay?" Hank asked.

Kalen shrugged. "A few days." His gaze shifted to a young man who placed a plastic bag on the bar top.

"Ah, here you go, Fawn," Bridget said, handing the bag to Faunalyn.

"Thanks again." Faunalyn gave Bridget and Hank a small wave. "I'll talk to you both soon. Have a good night."

Kalen stiffened slightly when Faunalyn took his hand and led him through the place and out the back door. Had it not been for the waves of warmth pummeling his head, he would've picked up on her tension a moment before she turned to face him.

"Next time, stay in the car."

Kalen's brows furrowed. "Didn't you ask if I wanted—"

"Yes, but"—she waved a hand—"ah, never mind. Let's go."

The ride to Faunalyn's small cottage in the woods was quiet except for soft music from the car stereo. Kalen tried to ignore the delicious aroma wafting from the bag of food, but the longer he basted in the aromatic air, the more his stomach begged for a tiny piece of something other than oatmeal or bland stews.

Every time he looked at the beautiful elf, he wanted more than a simple smile or an imaginary kiss.

Kalen jerked his gaze from Faunalyn, pressed his lips together, and tried to quench all forms of hunger that plagued him as he watched the dark houses and trees pass by.

You can't get caught up in this woman.

Not that he knew the first thing about getting *caught up* with a woman.

Faunalyn pulled down a dark dirt trail and parked her car beside her small home. She cast him a short glance before climbing from the car, grabbing up the bag of food, and closing the door behind her. He watched her walk to the front door before he realized he was probably expected to follow.

Taking her queue, he met Faunalyn at the front door and accepted her invitation into the house. Unlike his first visit, he took a long moment to observe her living quarters, noticing the greens and golds and browns that colored the main room. Plants and flowers grew lushly from pots positioned throughout the space. The kitchen counter had two small plants, ivy of some sort. The air smelled subtly sweet and exotic and immediately soothed his soul.

He had been in such a near panic after the accident that he had barely taken notice of any of these trivial details the first night. The more he soaked in Faunalyn's tastes and style, the more he felt her sink deeper than his mere senses. It was like the woman became his breath, the energy that gave him life. It made no sense.

It made absolute sense.

She unpacked boxes onto a small table. So beautiful. Stunning, really. She moved with a determined grace, each turn, stretch, shift of her body commanding his attention. Her subtle gestures, from the gentle furrow of her brow to the tug of her lower lip between her teeth, stirred a heat in his body he'd never before known. Her golden hair remained tied back from work, the thick waves catching the soft yellow light from the fancy ceiling light.

His fingers tingled. His entire *body* tingled.

Kalen moved to her side and caught a loose tendril of her hair in his hand.

Faunalyn gasped and jumped, spinning to stare at him with wide eyes. The very *un*graceful motion jerked the hair from his palm like a string of silk.

"Geez, sorry. You startled me. I'm not used to fae moving so quickly." Faunalyn laughed—the sound like a hypnotic melody—and a blush darkened her cheeks. "I have to remember that with you."

"I'm sorry. I didn't mean to frighten you." He truly didn't, and he didn't mean to end the revelation of her hair against his skin, either. "I forget I move differently at times."

Faunalyn leaned a hip against the edge of the table. "You don't realize you move like a vampire?"

Kalen shook his head. Before the escape, he never paid heed to his movements and how others perceived them. The Lab Coats often kept his strengths restrained with a regime of medications. It was Nicholas who warned him to be mindful of how he moved and to take caution to blend in with the humans.

"It will be easier for you to pull off being of fae descent rather than trying to explain the vampire traits that most mortals believe are nothing more than horror stories. Your ears can be explained as a birth defect. Your eyes, a rarity. But your speed and your senses? Far more difficult and convoluted. Best stay away from that."

Somehow, Faunalyn made him forget to be cautious. Forget his dire situation. Forget the darkness plaguing his sister. Forget himself.

That was dangerous.

She was dangerous.

"Would you be willing to tell me more about your past? Over burgers?" Faunalyn motioned to the boxes on the table. "I hope you don't mind. I ordered you a burger."

Kalen opened one of the boxes with a flick of magic and stared at the items it held. A burger, fries, and a piece of lettuce, tomato, and onion on the side. His mouth watered and his jaw tightened at the smell of food he'd only seen in movies.

"May I confide in you?"

His voice sounded alien even to his own ears. When he turned his gaze from the food, he noticed Faunalyn's eyes had softened to a beautiful shade of shimmering lavender-gold. Her brows lifted just a little, and he wasn't sure if it was pity or concern that touched the edges of her expression.

"Whatever you tell me, Kalen, stays between us. You can trust me."

Blast that word.

But coming from Faunalyn, he couldn't imagine the implied promise sounding any more genuine.

He nodded slowly, accepting her word. "I've never had a burger before."

Faunalyn stared at him for a long moment before her lips curled into a smile. "Really?" She laughed and pulled out a chair at the table. "Well, then. What are we waiting for? Howler's whips up a mean burger, so your deflowering of burger virginity is going to be spectacular."

Chapter 7

A little past three in the morning, and several yawns later, Fawn took Kalen up on calling it a night. He tried to insist she didn't have to drive him to Jackson's house, but she wasn't about to let him traipse through Nocturne Falls alone at this hour. Besides, his eyes were red-rimmed and the circles she noted under his eyes earlier in the evening had darkened. His pale skin looked almost translucent.

She took a quick shower after dinner—she never watched a person express such delight in a burger, and it made her realize how much people took for granted, even the joy of a shower—and changed into a pair of pajama shorts and a long-sleeved shirt. It was normal sleep attire for her and completely unsexy. Or so she thought, until she caught the darkened glow of Kalen's eyes as he looked her over. And over. It no longer felt like casual sleepwear.

The drive to Jackson's house was anything but relaxed, and it had everything to do with that single expression that took over Kalen's face.

Hunger.

Whether he understood it or not, Fawn knew a look that raw and primitive was not rooted in lust. She'd known *those* looks. She had her fair share of dates with *those* types of men.

Oh no.

Kalen's hunger was deep. So deep she felt it in her own spirit.

Nature elves didn't believe in soul mates, but they did believe connections between people and potential couples often presented in obscure ways. Car crashes and strange vampire-fae creatures might be considered obscure. She couldn't deny there was some connection between Kalen and herself. She'd be lying if she said she didn't feel something for the guy sitting next to her, as crazy as that sounded.

"Thank you for the burger."

Fawn snorted out a laugh as she pulled up to Jackson's house. "Don't mention it." When she caught the familiar confusion in his expression, she shook her head. "It's a figure of speech. Kinda like 'no problem' or 'it was nothing.' I'm glad you enjoyed it."

"I enjoyed a lot this evening. Mostly you."

Blunt sincerity. She appreciated that, even if it did make her blush. "Well, I'm happy to have given you some joy. From what you've shared with me, you haven't had much."

Not that he shared much outside of admitting to the things he didn't know or understand because he and his sister spent their lives locked up in rooms. She learned their meals weren't much more exciting than bland stews and porridge-like dishes. He received blood transfusions to keep his bloodlust from getting out of control. His ally, Nicholas, snuck in movies and videos to help acclimate him and Vivian to the world beyond the walls of their prison in preparation for an escape.

Kalen avoided talking about what happened in the labs. His shame was palpable whenever he mentioned testing or Lab Coats—as he and his sister came to call the medical personnel slash guards—and she didn't have the heart to press him about it.

"I hope that changes," Kalen said, his eyes meeting hers. "For Vivi and me."

Fawn didn't jump this time when his hand suddenly pressed to the side of her face, his palm molding to her cheek. His eyes narrowed slightly as his body turned toward her. The air between them thickened with restrained energy, making it difficult to breathe. Her heart raced. Electric prickles skittered along her skin from his touch, feeding into the heaviness of the moment.

"Forgive me." His voice had become a husk, both liquid heat and rough caress. Fawn's breath ceased the moment he leaned toward her. "I haven't done this before."

"Way-way-wait a minute." Fawn leaned back, a single finger shoved between their mouths. "You've never kissed a woman before?"

That adorable crease formed over his brows, the one that told her he was both uncertain and a little embarrassed.

"Other than my sister, no."

Fawn's eyes went wide. Kalen stared at her like what he said was the most normal thing to come from his mouth. However, his eyes belied his confusion.

Then his lips parted on a soft laugh. "Oh, I see. *Kiss*."

She sputtered, speechless as he leaned over and brushed an airy kiss to her cheek.

"Like that." He lifted his mouth to her forehead, landing another airy kiss on her skin. "And that. Those kisses." His thumb brushed over her lips, his fingers tipping her chin up. Her sputtering ceased when his mouth brushed over hers, a soft, gentle touch. A tease that sparked a dangerous heat in her belly. "But never like that."

"Well..." Her voice thickened until she could speak in nothing more than a desire-laced whisper. "That's good."

His stormy gaze held hers for a long moment, leaving her with the impression he was peeling back layers around her soul, searching for something, not understanding but following simple instinct.

Until this moment, Fawn kept her wits about her, locking away her uncharacteristic desires in the presence of Kalen.

Until this moment, Fawn had complete control over her emotions.

A barrier fractured, splintered, and gave way. She reached for his face, cupping it between her hands, and drew him back for another kiss. Their lips lingered for some time, anticipation skyrocketing.

Then, Fawn gently parted her lips and tasted the seam of his mouth with the tip of her tongue.

Kalen's finger slid back into her hair, fisting against her scalp. A sharp exhale fled his mouth, filling her lungs with the raw essence of him. She stole the opportunity, indulging in a slow, cautious kiss, tasting him, learning him, and realized after only a couple of sweeps of her tongue he was a damn fast learner.

And a damn amazing kisser.

A soft moan rolled off her tongue as he took control of the kiss, impressing his hunger on her with each fulfilling plunder. Each kiss became a potent mix of restraint and desire, a battle between tender and carnal. Fawn inched closer, wrapping an arm around his neck, raking a hand into the soft satin of his hair. She relished the guttural sound that resonated from his chest a second before his kiss turned possessive.

And she thoroughly enjoyed it.

A knock echoed through the car.

Kalen jerked back with a hiss. Fawn caught the shimmer of half extended fangs as he twisted toward the sound. Jackson peered at them through Fawn's window. He pushed his glasses onto the bridge of his nose, his face dark with color and shadows. At least he had the decency to look away.

Caught up in the haze of Kalen's kiss, it took Fawn a few seconds longer to realize the man appeared more worried than he should for interrupting them in a simple kiss.

"What do you want?" Kalen snapped.

Fawn rested a hand on Kalen's shoulder. "Something's wrong."

She jumped out of the car, but Kalen had taken off like a ghost, disappearing into the house. Fawn tried her hardest to ignore the pleasant throb of her lips and the taste of Kalen filling her mouth.

"What is it?" she asked.

Jackson shrugged, his eyes glinting with helplessness. "I don't know. Vivian is freaking out. The sedative was supposed to hold her until afternoon. A lower dose has kept her calm for more than twelve hours."

Fawn cringed when she heard a piercing shriek from inside the house, followed by a crash. Her attention flew to the neighboring house, which remained dark.

She wasn't sure if she had what it would take to calm the frantic woman again, especially within a house, but she was willing to try. If the neighbors woke and called the sheriff's department, Kalen and Vivian would find themselves in more danger than they needed right now.

She glanced at Jackson before running to the front door. Jackson followed at her heels, hissing warnings at her not to go in. Leave Vivian to Kalen. She couldn't.

Kalen, as much as he was Vivian's brother, had little control over this monster. At least, that's what she believed after witnessing Vivian's behavior following the accident.

Another loud crash shook the house. She bolted down the hallway and came to a halt in the doorway of a bedroom where Kalen was trying to talk sense into a wild-eyed, fanged Vivian.

Fawn had half a second to come up with a plan before Vivian's crazed gaze snapped to her. The woman lunged a blink later.

"Vivian, no!" Kalen barked.

Fawn saw nothing but a blur of color before pain shot up and down her body as she slammed into the wall across the hallway, and her head filled with stars. She managed to whip a hand up to cover her throat. Vivian's needle-like teeth sank into the back of her hand. She sucked in a breath at the pain, but used the precious seconds of distraction to call up the magic of her people from the depths of her spirit. She barely noticed Kalen pull at his sister's waist, trying to dislodge her teeth from Fawn's hand, before the familiar warmth of power and magic filled every cell in her body.

Fawn flattened her free palm on Vivian's chest and expelled the glorious bright magic into the woman.

Vivian gasped, jerked, then went boneless. Her teeth retracted and she crumpled into a ball on the floor.

Kalen touched his sister's cheek before his attention shot to Fawn. "What do you do to calm her? You *must* show me."

Fawn tried to hide the damage to her hand, but Kalen snatched it before she could tuck it behind her leg. His lips tightened and regret etched his expression.

When he touched the torn skin, she winced. She doubted Vivian's bite pierced her clean, and wondered about possible damage to the tendons or bone.

"Don't move, Faunalyn," Kalen murmured, leaning back on his heels. He scooped Vivian up in his arms and disappeared into the bedroom. Jackson sighed as he knelt at Fawn's side and examined her hand.

"I detect a fracture," Jackson said, shaking his head. By the throbbing pain, she didn't doubt him. "I told you to stay outside. Kalen can handle her."

"Didn't look that way," Fawn said, lifting her head to the doorway. "What happened?"

Kalen appeared in front of her. He took her hand from Jackson and brushed a mussed lock of hair from her face. "We've been subjected to experiments to try and create daywalkers—vampires who can tolerate the sunlight and not become ash. Jackson is trying to unravel the coding of the restructured DNA they injected into my sister. Whatever they did, it's killing her. Killing the fae in her, feeding it to a monster. Their experiment went wrong, and they couldn't fix it. They were going to put her down the night we escaped. Nicholas helped us get out of the facility to save Vivi. She's grown sensitive to sunlight and we could only move at night. Nicholas was supposed to come with us. He and Jackson were going to figure out a cure."

Fawn stared, aghast. "They were going to *kill* your sister?"

Kalen nodded, lowering his gaze to her hand. "Yes. She injured one of the scientists and they realized they'd lost control of their test subject. As much as they wanted us for their experiments, they didn't need two subjects. Vivi was disposable. Nicholas sedated her and convinced the team to give him time alone with her to see if he could reverse the mistake, or virus, whatever it was. That was when we escaped."

"Have you had any success?" Fawn asked Jackson.

The man shrugged. "I've found possible structural issues in Vivian's cells, but I still need to figure out how to penetrate the viral coat and fix the coding to replace the damaged DNA with good DNA. Problem is, the bad is killing the good faster than I can research and experiment. And my personal lab here has limited equipment."

Fawn's stomach rolled. She hadn't realized how desperate the situation was. She knew it had to be bad, but never imaged it was life or death. And death hovered like an ominous cloud over Vivian's head.

"Will you allow me to heal you?" Kalen asked, his thumb running tenderly over her bleeding wound.

The adrenaline that drove Fawn to call up her power fled. Her eyelids grew heavy. All she wanted to do was curl up and fall asleep on the floor. She'd regret it in the morning, but right now it sounded like paradise.

"Yes, you may," Fawn said, shifting to get her feet beneath her. Kalen stood and helped her up, his arm supporting her around the waist while he held her injured hand. Jackson straightened, too, and cleared his throat.

"Do you need any bandages, Kalen?" he asked.

"No."

"Actually, yes," Fawn said. At Kalen's arched brow, she grinned.

"I'll be right back." Jackson started one way down the hall, then paused, turned, and headed the opposite direction. They watched as he disappeared into another room.

Fawn pressed a finger to Kalen's mouth the moment he opened it. "Don't. I know you're going to apologize for her, but don't. She's not at fault and it's just a small bite."

Kalen's shoulders dropped. The emotions that took over his expression and caused his eyes to dim tore into Fawn. His helplessness resonated against her spirit. His fear of losing his sister.

"Listen. Give me a few minutes with her, okay? You can heal the wound when I'm done. Why don't you go into the living room and I'll be right there." She wasn't entirely sure what she was going to do, but she needed a few minutes alone with Vivian once her hand was bandaged. "I promise."

The circles under Kalen's eyes and the paleness of his skin had intensified over the last ten minutes. She wondered how much of that had to do with his need for blood, and how much was due to his beleaguered spirit.

"I don't want her to hurt you again," he said quietly.

Fawn smiled. "She won't."

Kalen considered her for a long minute. In that time, Jackson reappeared, bandages in one hand and what looked like a phlebotomy kit in the other. Fawn reached for the bandages, but Kalen grabbed the roll of gauze and small package of gauze squares first. Jackson held up the butterfly needle, tubing, and vial in his other hand.

"I'm going to draw a sample of her blood. I want to look at it under a microscope and see if whatever Fawn did is having an effect on Vivi beyond the magical," Jackson said, not slowing as he walked into Vivian's bedroom.

Kalen rubbed the back of his neck, the stiff movement one of unease.

"Which is bothering you more? The needle or the scent of my blood?" Fawn finally asked, keeping her voice low. Kalen's gaze sharpened and snapped back to her. "How often do you need blood? And when was the last time you had some?"

Kalen pressed his lips together. His gaze dropped to the items in his hand. Without answering, he opened one of the square packages and pulled out the gauze pads. Fawn didn't take her eyes off his face as he made quick work of cleaning the back of her hand and wrapping it. Through the entire process, she watched his expression strain to remain in control, his eyes taking on a hint of glowing blue.

She took his hand before he pulled away and drew up enough strength from the Earth to pour a sense of calm into him. Kalen's eyes widened and his lips parted on a soft gasp. His fingers curled around hers like a man desperately holding on to the last thread of hope.

"I'm going to help you, Kalen. You and Vivian. I need you to be honest with me, though. I can't help if I don't know what to do."

Jackson came out of Vivian's room and raised the vial of blood. "I'm going to test this out and see if there are any clues. If you need me, I'll be in my lab."

Kalen twisted enough to watch Jackson until the guy disappeared behind another door.

"I was transfused twice a week at the lab. Nicholas said I didn't need blood that often. It was more of a precaution than a necessity. I haven't had blood in almost a week." He closed his eyes. "And I thirst."

His confession was tinged with shame. She couldn't begin to imagine his suffering. She pressed up on her toes and kissed his cheek.

"You're in a paranormal town. There are resources here. Let me see what I can do."

"No. I'll manage."

"You'll manage until you can't. And at that point, it'll be too late." She stepped back. "I won't be long with Vivian."

"You will call for me if you need anything."

"I will. Promise."

Fawn moved toward Vivian's room. He didn't try to stop her—a good sign, she supposed—but he watched closely as she took another step into the room. When she turned away from him, she felt the heat of his gaze against her back, and she quietly closed the door.

Vivian lay on the bed hunched in the fetal position, still as stone. Her shoulder didn't move the slightest with any sign of breathing. Did she need to breathe?

Fawn rounded the bed and knelt beside the silent woman. Her lips were closed, hiding any evidence of her fangs. Her cheeks were sallow and gray and dark circles stretched to her eyelids. She looked frail in the oversized sweatshirt and sweatpants.

"I'm sorry."

Vivian's apology was so quiet, had Fawn not seen the small movement of her lips, she wouldn't have believed the woman spoke at all.

"I hope you don't mind me coming in here."

Vivian's eyes opened to mere slits, but the brilliant blue of her irises glowed like beacons in a pitch-black night.

A spirit reaching out from inside a monster for help.

As the thought crossed her mind, the reality of Vivian's circumstances left her momentarily breathless.

"No. My brother remains close."

Fawn nodded. "I haven't seen such dedication from a sibling." She settled back on her heels, her small smile fading as a shot of pain demanded her attention. "How is it I'm able to subdue you? This is twice now. Tell me what it feels like."

Vivian lifted her head enough to tuck her arm beneath it. Her eyes opened completely to reveal irises as bright and stunning as her brother's.

"I don't know. Whatever you do, it leaves me free of the darkness. It tires me terribly, but..." Vivian pressed her lips together. Fawn swore she caught a slight tremor along her chin. "I feel like my old self again. Like I have control again. Whatever magic you use jumpstarts my memory and brings me back to, well, me."

Fawn rested her uninjured hand over Vivian's. She was surprised by how cool her skin felt compared to Kalen's.

"Kalen told me some of what's been going on. I want to help."

Vivian was silent for a long time, her eyes wandering over Fawn curiously. She dipped her head, cast her eyes toward the door, then returned to Fawn.

"I want my brother to be happy." Vivian smiled sadly. "I know my fate, but he is unwilling to accept it. I want him to live. For us both. I *need* him to live. And it seems fate brought him to you for that purpose."

Fawn's heart broke at the woman's acceptance of a fate unknown. It ate her up thinking Vivian was still so young in both fae and vampire years, and she was willing to give up.

"Whatever the gods have in mind, I can promise you I will do whatever I can to help." Because *she* wasn't willing to resign herself to failure. The promise came from the depths of her soul. So what if Kalen's kiss might have put a pinch more passion behind her promise? "Is there anything I can get for you?"

Vivian shook her head. "I'm tired. He waits to heal you."

Fawn took her leave, closing the door behind her. She found Kalen in the living room, hands in his pockets, staring out the window through a gauzy curtain. The lights remained off in the room, and the faint glow of the street lamps cast him in beautiful silhouette. She couldn't help but stare. He was absolute perfection, and she'd shamelessly enjoy these silent moments.

"I will not accept her perceived outcome. I can't. She doesn't understand that."

His voice was soft, strained, flooded with emotion that wrung her chest into a tight knot. She quietly crossed the room to stand behind him. To think, three days ago, she had a routine, a schedule, a passion that started in her garden and ended at her smoothie shop. To think just this morning, she woke up like any other day, never expecting it to end with a bite on her hand, a kiss from a god, and a determination to make the world of two near strangers better.

"I made a promise. To protect her."

"And you continue to keep your promise."

Kalen turned away from the window. His gaze landed on her, as soft as the brush of his fingers over her lips. The intimate motion should have sent her reeling—he took liberties she would never allow a guy to take after a single meal—instead of leaning closer.

She blamed the droop of her eyelids on her fatigue.

"I should heal your wound."

Fawn nodded. Distraction was good.

Unfortunately, what she hoped would have been a distraction only proved to her how quickly she was becoming enthralled by a vampire-fae man who needed a lesson in modern living and a miracle to remain alive.

Chapter 8

Another sleepless night. His sixth in a row. Sleep evaded him, his worry for Vivian growing by the day. He remained by her bedside after Faunalyn left. He tried to convince the elf to stay, worried she would not make it home safely. He realized shortly after she had gone that he ached at their separation and part of his disappointment in her decision to leave was based solely on a selfish need to have her close.

Standing vigil over his sister always reverted his attention to his cause.

Except for tonight.

Vivian slept and Kalen's mind wandered to Faunalyn. Everything about her, from her grace and kindness to that kiss, sucked him in. As the sun rose over the horizon, bringing its flare of stunning colors, he counted down the hours until Faunalyn's shop opened.

The only thing that distracted him from Faunalyn was meeting Jackson in the kitchen, the other man ruffled from sleep with his glasses set haphazardly on his nose and his hair its usual mess. He yawned as he shuffled to the coffee pot, popped a *pod* into the top, and brewed himself a cup. Kalen watched the man, eating a muffin he found in the pantry.

"Well, I think we might have a little breakthrough," Jackson said, his back to Kalen. Kalen paused with a piece of muffin in his fingers, and straightened in his chair. "Whatever Fawn did to your sister, it seemed to have paralyzed the progression of the virus. It may explain why the sedative was working until last night. Fawn's magic must've worn off. With her help, it'll buy some time to try and fix this mess."

Kalen remained quiet, caught in the potent memory of a subtle wave of heat flowing into his body from Faunalyn's touch while he struggled to contain the thirst of the vampire. Whatever magic she used on him suppressed the hunger, that blood thirst he was so unfamiliar with.

One thought became a living beacon. One that frightened him as much as it exhilarated him.

"You have nothing to say? I was expecting something. A shout. A hoot. Maybe some fist-bumping."

Kalen's brows rose.

Jackson shrugged. "A grin?"

He gave Jackson a grin. This news was exciting and filled him with hope. His only question was, at what expense? He would do anything to save his sister. Anything, except betray Faunalyn.

"You should probably talk to Fawn and let her know. See if she'd be willing to continue using her magic on Vivian. I'm making headway on the notes my uncle sent on the flash drive. They're bits and pieces of the testing and lab reports. It's tedious, time-consuming work. If I had some *help*..."

Kalen scowled, dropping the muffin on the plate. He abruptly stood and brushed his hands against his jeans. "We were ambushed. There was nothing I could do."

"I don't mean my uncle. I'm just saying if I had another set of eyes to help me, I'd get through this a lot faster. I'm only part witch, and barely at that. I'm all geek."

Kalen hadn't a clue what he meant by geek, but figured it had something to do with his scientific equipment.

"What do you propose we do, Jackson? Tell people who might contact the lab and give us away?"

"No one will contact the lab." Jackson sipped his coffee, his eyes sharpening with each second. "I think we need more manpower. Just one more person."

"*No.*" Kalen spun on his heel and left the room before Jackson could put up an argument. He stopped by Vivian's room. His sister was curled up as she had been since he placed her in the bed. He went to his room, changed into a fresh set of clothing and took off to find Faunalyn.

Her smoothie store was locked, the Closed sign in place, and the interior dressed in shadows. He checked the time against the watch Jackson let him borrow, a sense of concern rising. She should have opened the shop over two hours earlier. The one thing he gathered about Faunalyn in the last couple of days spent watching her was her precision and responsibility.

A few humans cut in front of him and stopped at the shop's door. One girl pressed her face to the window and peered inside.

"Do you think it'll be open later?" the girl asked. An older woman shrugged.

"I don't know. We can check back, honey. Let's keep moving."

Kalen looked up and down the sidewalk, which was mobbed with a mix of humans and paranormals, some dressed in costumes, others in regular clothing. The street was jammed with cars moving slowly, trolling for parking spots, filled with tourists gaping at the storefronts. He would come back in a little while and wait for her if he couldn't find Faunalyn elsewhere.

He checked the coffee shop she had introduced him to. No beautiful elf. He meandered into a clothing store, a candy shop, an ice cream shop—he made a mental note to return there to indulge—and a hat shop. Over an hour spent walking and searching resulted in nothing.

He nearly passed by a flower store called Enchanted Garden when an idea came to mind.

The shop had a few customers, but it wasn't as packed as most of the other places he'd stopped in.

Keeping to the perimeter of the room, he headed straight to the glass doors that showcased bouquets of premade arrangements.

A pretty woman with blond hair came to him a few minutes later. "Looking for a special gift?"

Kalen shrugged. Even though he kept his sunglasses in place, he didn't look at the woman for long. "How much do those run?"

"The small ones start at twenty-five dollars and they run up to a hundred. Or I can make you something custom. It all depends on what you're looking for. Is it for a special lady?"

Twenty-five dollars? Nicholas had supplied him with cash, but it certainly wasn't much. It was enough to get by for a few weeks. He had told Kalen once they cured Vivian, he wouldn't have to worry about money. His mentor never explained more.

"How much is a single rose?"

"Long-stemmed are five dollars."

"I'll take one."

The woman smiled as she opened one of the glass doors. "Is there a specific color?"

Kalen looked over the buckets of roses. Red, pink, white. He pointed to a stunning yellow rose. "That one. It's perfect."

"You have good taste." The woman drew the rose from the bucket and closed the door. "Anything else?"

"Just the rose."

Cellophane-wrapped gift in hand, Kalen checked back at the smoothie shop to see if Faunalyn had arrived. The lights remained off in front, but he noticed a sliver of dim light in the back room. He made his way to the rear of the store after checking the front door—still locked—and tested his luck with the back door.

To his relief, it was open, and he slipped in silently.

He made it two steps before an airy melody froze him in place. His head buzzed as he listened to the beautiful song, soft words and fluid notes captivating him. Calm, serenity, assurance. The flowing voice produced such magic in a language he knew nothing of. His entire body weakened and relaxed. His heart, the slow beating organ in his chest that rarely reacted to anything, thumped to a flutter. A humming sensation started at the base of his throat as a warm tingle poured over his skin.

Faunalyn's voice dipped, then rose like a subtle wave on a body of water. Her song lapped along his mind, coasted over his body, and settled in the last place he ever expected.

A bright, pulsing light. Deep within his soul.

Kalen couldn't shake the sensations, but he somehow managed to free his limbs from her entrancing song. A powerful drive brought him up behind her in a small room cluttered with papers and files and boxes.

"Faunalyn," he whispered.

Faunalyn spun with a gasp. A gasp he quickly drank into his lungs when he kissed her. The moment his lips pressed hard to hers, he realized his mistake.

Until her arms wrapped around his neck and she responded to each hungry sweep of his tongue.

Maybe his forward action wasn't such a mistake after all.

He listened to her sweet moans, reacted to the press of her body against his, drowned in the crescendo of waves that left him flailing mindlessly.

Oh, how soft her skin was. How lovely her neck tasted. How…

Kalen jerked back, swallowing down the throbbing ache in his gums from his extended incisors.

Faunalyn cupped his face between her hands. Sweet goddess, did he do that to her lips? Make them so sexy and swollen? Did he cause her cheeks to flush with blood and her eyes to flare?

"One time," she murmured, her thumb tracing his upper lip. Her nail brushed the tip of his fang. "It'll be okay one time."

It took him a moment to realize what she was offering. The haze that consumed him left little space for him to think clearly, but he knew he could not take what she so selflessly offered.

Kalen groaned, lowering his head. "I can't."

"Why?"

"I don't want to hurt you." Truth was, he'd never bitten into a neck before, and feared he'd cause her far more pain than he cared to. He'd starve himself of blood before Faunalyn gained another injury on his behalf. To distract himself from the potent taste of her mouth and the sudden, unrelenting desire to pick up where they left off, he pulled his arm back and presented her with the rose he held tightly in his hand. "I brought you a gift."

Faunalyn's eyes lit up, as did the smile that crossed her mouth. She took the rose and brought it to her nose, inhaling deeply. "It's beautiful." She raised her eyes to him. "Thank you."

Kalen cleared his throat. "I didn't mean to startle you before. That song was…it was…" He stepped back, trying to get a handle on his thoughts. "You shouldn't leave your back door unlocked."

Her eyes narrowed, but her smile widened. "If I have to worry about you sneaking in and kissing me mad, then I'll be sure to lock it."

Kalen caught the edge of humor in her voice and let out a rusty chuckle. "You may be well off doing so."

"Are you flirting with me?"

"I think I skipped this flirting you speak of. That comes before the mad kiss, doesn't it?" He was pretty sure it did. He drew his fingers along her chin, wanting so badly to kiss her. "But I'll be more than happy to kiss you again."

"I'd like that."

He obliged, taking his time, breathing in her scent, soaking in the flavor of sweetness from her lips. His fingers sank into her hair, curling along her scalp. He tipped her head back a little more until he could kiss her fully and was pleasantly surprised when she sighed and arched into him.

He may know little about this woman, but his soul felt as if they'd known each other for ages. She felt right. She felt safe. She felt perfect.

When he ended the kiss, he held her tight as she swayed.

"I think you've been dishonest with me about never kissing a woman," she murmured, her voice thick and utterly enthralling.

"I've been nothing but honest," Kalen said. True, although obscured. "I came here to talk to you. Seems I've forgotten to do so. I don't want to hold you up while you open your store."

Faunalyn shook her head. "I'm remaining closed today. I stopped by to get the mail, put away the deliveries, and pick up my invoices so I can pay them from home." She pointed to the pile of papers on her desk. "Some things came up."

"If you have time today, I'd like to tell you about Vivian."

"I have time. Come on. Let me lock up and we'll head back to my place." She nudged him with her elbow. "I'll make you something to eat."

"Only if I can have your tea."

"You can have all the tea you'd like."

"Amazing," Kalen said on a breath as he sat back in the chair. He washed down the last of his food—Faunalyn had called the meat and bread stacks club sandwiches—with her fresh brewed floral tea and sighed. He felt her gaze on him throughout their late lunch, and often looked up to catch her eyes. Those moments of intense silence, staring at each other, created an energy that sizzled along his nerves. "I need to learn to cook like this so I can repay your generosity."

"Well, how about after things are settled with Vivian, I teach you a few things in the kitchen. Would you like that?" Faunalyn asked, folding her hands over her plate. The yellow rose sat in a slim vase between them, the sunlight casting it in a beautiful golden glow. So close to the color of her hair.

"I'd like that." He honestly would. He needed to learn so much about this world, how to survive independently. Cooking was a skill he'd never learned. Neither was banking or money handling or doing laundry. Learning to cook alongside Faunalyn would be pure bliss.

Learning Faunalyn would be pure bliss.

The sample of what she felt like under his hands—the curve of her hip, the arch of her lower back, the firmness of her legs—left him craving more.

"So, tell me about Vivian. Is she doing better this morning?"

Kalen dabbed at the corner of his mouth with his napkin and nodded once. "Yes. She was sleeping quietly when I left. Jackson studied the blood sample he took last night. He said the virus—it's what he's calling the defective coding of her DNA—exhibited paralysis after the magic you used on her. Whatever you did helped slow the progress of the virus."

Faunalyn's lips parted on a gasp. "Really? Well, if I can help through my magic, do you think Jackson will be able to find a cure and reverse the damage?"

Kalen's lips curled on their own accord. "I had wanted to ask if you'd be willing to offer your assistance."

She sat up straight, a faint crease forming over her brows. "Of course! If it'll help her, of—"

A loud knock interrupted Faunalyn's enthusiastic reply and immediately put Kalen on edge. He glanced at the door, then back at Faunalyn.

"Give me a minute."

He waited until she was halfway to the door before he grabbed his plate, napkin, and glass, quietly left them in the kitchen, and ducked into a room down the hallway. His movements were at vampire speed, stealthy and silent. He didn't want anyone to know he was here, or that Faunalyn was associated with him. Not until he knew for certain he and Vivian were out of danger.

The last time he let his guard down, Nicholas ended up dead.

As Kalen waited for Faunalyn to answer the door, he looked over the room he'd dipped in to. A knot tightened low in his belly as his eyes landed on a bed draped in soft blankets of lavender and rose. White lace curtains let in plenty of light. The vases of flowers on the nightstand and dresser lent a luscious scent to the room, one he had detected lingering in Faunalyn's hair.

He squeezed his eyes shut and rested his head against the wall. He should've found the bathroom instead of her room. The woman plagued him every which way to impossible. Now he could easily picture her sleeping on that bed. Sleeping in those tiny shorts and cute top.

Or none of those items.

"Sorry to bother you, Fawn. I stopped by the store, but you were closed. Is everything okay?"

The deep, gruff voice he recognized as Hank Merrow's. His stomach performed a sickening twist.

"Yeah. Some things came up, that's all."

"I've never known your store to stay closed since you moved here."

"I'm overdue for a call-out." Faunalyn's airy laugh did little to cut through the growing heaviness of the air within the small cottage. "What can I help you with?"

"I wanted to talk to you. About that accident from a few nights ago."

"Of course. I'm not sure I'll be much help, but I'll do what I can."

Kalen's fingers balled into fists as he slowed his breathing to nothing. His heart beat a couple of times a minute. He was a virtual statue. He knew now what the sheriff and his sister were. He hoped the wolf traipsing into Faunalyn's house wouldn't pick up his scent.

"I'm not interrupting your lunch, am I?" the sheriff asked.

"No. I was just about through."

Kalen heard the faint hesitation in her words. As each moment passed, he wondered if he should've stayed at the table, like a man who had nothing to hide from the law.

"Can I get you a drink?"

"Nah. I'll only be a few minutes. Are you sure you didn't see anyone run from that car? No one, say, ran through your yard or knocked on your door?"

"No. Not that I saw or heard. Why? Have you found out anything more about the owner of the car?"

"We were finally able to trace it to its owner. A Nicholas Tennerston."

"That's good. I'm sure he'd like to know where his car is, if it was stolen."

"I'm sure he'd like to know, too." The sheriff was silent, and in that silence, Kalen's panic began to rise. If they'd traced that car to Nicholas, then... "If Tennerston wasn't dead."

Fawn's exhalation of surprise sounded forced to Kalen as she said, "Oh no."

"I spoke with the sheriff's department out of Tennessee where they located his body. He was murdered about four days ago. The only contact was a Dr. Hamstead. I've been in touch with him and he's headed down here tomorrow. Gave me a little information about the possible suspects. I'm concerned they might be lingering in the forest by your house, and that you might be in danger."

"If you don't mind me asking, what happened to the car's owner?"

Kalen cringed, swallowing back the sudden swell of anger that roiled through his chest.

"Hamstead warned me that the suspects are loose canons. Paranormals of a dangerous kind. The victim was found mauled in a hotel room."

The gasp that came from Faunalyn's mouth was anything but an act. Kalen realized instantly how this made him look. His sister look. Dr. Hamstead was making them out to be crazed vampires.

His fangs pierced his lower lip. He held a hiss behind clenched teeth.

"This...doctor was forthcoming about these suspects' paranormal origins. People don't throw around paranormal encounters like casual talk. They run the risk of looking nuts."

Kalen placed the sheriff in the house as the wolf's heavy-booted steps came closer to the hallway.

"Well, I have one link to Tennerston here in Nocturne Falls. A distant relative. I'll be following up with him when I leave here. I don't need any bodies showing up in this town. If you hear of anything, call me. We need to get these two off the streets and back into the custody of this Hamstead fellow. I'm serious, Fawn. I don't want harm to come to you."

"I appreciate your concern. If anything comes along, I'll let you know."

"Well, have a good day."

Kalen didn't blink until he heard the sound of tires crunching over dirt and rock. He rolled off the wall and into the hallway as Faunalyn stepped in front of him.

"We have to get to your sister," she said urgently, grabbing his wrist. "Do you know Jackson's number?"

"Aren't you concerned about what the sheriff told you?"

"I'm concerned that you're being framed to look like a murderer."

Kalen tugged his arm back, causing Faunalyn to pause and look at him. "How can you be sure I'm not?"

He shouldn't press his luck. Not with her, the only ally he and his sister had besides Jackson. But he needed to know why she placed her trust in him.

The adorable crease in her forehead returned. Her eyes filled with a flood of emotion. "I've seen the way you are with your sister, Kalen. I've listened to the admiration in your voice when you speak of Nicholas. I watch how you interact with Jackson." She sighed. "You would've protected Nicholas had your sister attacked him. Just as you did for me, and I'm practically a stranger. You've turned away from my offer to feed even though you thirst. You have more dignity and control than most, but right now, we need to get to your sister."

"Stay here. I'll be back soon."

Before she could argue, Kalen bolted from the house, using vampire speed to reach Jackson's house before the sheriff arrived. He slowed only after he threw open the front door.

Jackson jumped up from the sofa in the living room when he stormed by, heading straight to Vivian's room.

"Kalen, geez! No running in the house," Jackson grumbled. "What's the rush?"

Vivian jerked upright in her bed, her eyes glowing blue beneath strands of pale hair. Kalen rested a hand on her shoulder.

"How do you feel, Vivi?" he asked quietly. She blinked once. "Do you feel in control?"

She gave a slight nod. "What has you panicked, brother?"

Jackson shuffled to the opposite side of the bed. "Yeah. That answer would be helpful."

"I was at Faunalyn's when the sheriff showed up. They've made the connection between the car and Nicholas." Kalen looked at Jackson. "Nicholas and you. Dr. Hamstead is expected to arrive tomorrow. It's just a matter of time before they launch a full-scale hunt. I need to hide you, Vivi. The sheriff is heading here now."

Jackson cussed under his breath. He raked both hands through his mussed hair. "Okay, umm, well…"

Kalen lifted his sister into his arms. "I need to get her out of this house. We can't stay here. If the connection between you and Nicholas was made, then Hamstead will certainly keep surveillance on this house once he arrives. It's not safe for you or us to remain."

"Kalen, you can't leave. Where will you go? With what funds? You don't have enough money for a room at a hotel or a bed-and-breakfast in town. And you can't abandon the opportunity to save Vivian. Listen." Jackson started pacing, his hands tugging at his hair. "Hide in the storage shed out back until Sheriff Merrow leaves. We'll figure out a safe place for you. Maybe Fawn can suggest something."

"I don't think you understand. If you're associated with me, Dr. Hamstead will not hesitate to harm you in order to make Vivian and I look like monsters. We lost Nicholas because he helped us. I'm not willing to lose any more innocents to this beast." Kalen's top lip curled in a scowl. "You need to tell the sheriff we held you captive so he will put you under his protection."

"Hey, Kal. I'm a big boy, and so was my uncle. He knew the dangers from the beginning, and so do I. I can make decisions for myself. I'm in this, whether you like it or not. I'm not going to give up trying to help you guys. You're stuck with me. You need to trust someone, Kalen. You can trust me, even when things get bad. My uncle wouldn't have helped you if he didn't think good would come out of righting your situation."

Kalen looked down at his sister and was surprised to find her eyes shimmering with tears. She tucked her head against his shoulder.

When he lifted his gaze to Jackson, the man raised his hand and shrugged. "So? Are you going to stand here all day or are you going to play hide-and-seek and head to the shed?"

Chapter 9

Fawn paced. Never in her life had she paced, but after attempting to find solace in her gardens, in song, and in sunlight, she cracked. Worry possessed her, such a cruel torture. She had no way of calling Kalen—did he even have a cell phone?—or reaching out to Jackson. Aside from knowing where Jackson lived, she had no information about him.

Hours passed and still nothing. The sky began its shift from crystal clear day to the sharp strokes of colored dusk. She showered, changed, did another walk through her gardens, but returned to her kitchen and the single rose in the vase on her table.

At last, she gave in to the maddening worry, snatched up her keys and purse, and stormed to the door.

Jackson stood on the stoop, fist raised to knock. His eyes widened as he stumbled back. Fawn grabbed his arm to steady him and looked around for any sign of Kalen.

"Is he okay? Are they okay?" she asked on short breaths. Her heart thundered. Did her body tremble? Oh, dear gods.

Jackson adjusted his glasses and cleared his throat. "They're in the car, but things are bad."

Fawn spotted the dark sedan parked silently off the dirt path leading to her house. The shadows of the approaching evening obscured it within the trees and brush.

The passenger door opened and Kalen climbed out, once more in dark clothing and a familiar hooded jacket.

"*How* bad?" Fawn asked. Her heart tore. How much more would Kalen and Vivian have to endure? They'd already survived a lifetime of misery. Wasn't that enough?

"Hamstead is a parasitic maniac. He will not stop hunting them until he has them. I need to get them out of Nocturne Falls. It's the only way to keep them safe. My grandmother has a cabin about an hour from here. I think it'll be safe until the good scientist realizes they're not here."

Fawn felt Jackson's words like a blow to her gut. The breath fled her. She looked at Kalen again. He lowered his head, but not before she caught the grim downturn of his lips.

How was it she'd known this man for little more than a few days and the news of him leaving town ripped down her middle?

He was brought to you by stronger powers. He is meant to be in your life, that's why.

Jackson sighed. He held up a bulging bag the size of a small suitcase. "I don't want to ask this of you, Fawn, I really don't, but I don't know who else I can trust. It's my laptop, some of my lab equipment, a copy of the USBs my uncle sent to me, and a copy of all the notes and documentation from my uncle and from me. If something happens to me, or to us, I need to know I can clear their names. Most of the stuff is circumstantial, but it's damning."

Fawn blinked. She shook her head to free it from the haze that started to settle. "No." She jerked back, shedding the haze completely. "No, you're not running away."

"But—"

She tilted her head and narrowed her eyes at Jackson. "How long have you lived here?"

"Six years."

"And in those six years, have you learned nothing about the people of this town? Geez." Fawn snatched the bag from his hand and motioned to the car. "Bring them in here."

Gentle hands came down on her shoulders as she started back into her house. That touch sent sparks and tingles along her skin and tried to battle the adrenaline pumping stronger and stronger in her system. She pressed her lips together, gathered her strength, and looked up as Kalen stepped in front of her.

"I will not put you in any danger, Faunalyn. I...can't," he murmured. Pain stabbed through his beautiful eyes. "I don't want Jackson in danger, either, but he refuses to listen to reason. One day, I'm certain, I'll be able to return."

"You won't do this alone. You've been through enough. I can't think of you enduring more pain, more misery."

"I've endured plenty enough that has made me strong. I may not wear the results on my skin, sweet Faunalyn, but they're there. Sometimes the scars are not on the surface. Sometimes they're hidden so deep even the wearer of those scars forgets they exist." The corner of his mouth twitched. His thumb brushed over her cheek. "I would never forgive myself if you got tangled up in this and harm came to you. That is one scar I couldn't bear to endure."

Fawn stared at him for a long time, reading the inner turmoil flooding his expression and filling his eyes. His skin had become so translucent he appeared almost ethereal. A manifestation more than a man. It pained her and piqued her interest about his fae origins.

She glanced around his arm. Jackson had returned to his car and waited by the open rear passenger door. Fawn pulled Kalen into her house and closed the door. She twisted back to him, lowering the bag to the floor, took his face in her hands, and brought him down for a soft kiss. She leaned back before it turned hot and caught his eyes.

"I want you to drink from me." She held a finger to his mouth the moment he started to protest. "Shh. You have been going without any blood for too long, and who knows how much longer it'll be before you can feed. I'm offering. Please. It'll make me feel better knowing you have more of your strength back. Let me help you."

She pleaded with him from the bottom of her heart. His brows furrowed at the same time the tips of his fangs became visible beneath his upper lip. His breathing, which was always slow and steady, turned to shallow gasps.

When his pupils swelled, blacking out the radiant blue of his eyes, she knew he would agree.

"You have done so much for me and Vivi." His voice was strained, a sexual blend of hunger, husk, and desire. "I've never fed—"

Fawn silenced him with a chaste kiss. She tilted her head, exposing her neck, and urged him down. Warmth flowed up through her feet and legs, a bright golden warmth of magic as she drew on the Earth to calm her and settle Kalen. His muscles, moments ago tense and hard, relaxed. His lips brushed her neck. Shots of pleasure filled her body and skewed her thoughts. Oh, how she wanted more than a kiss from Kalen.

The razor points of his teeth scraped her skin. She combed her fingers through his hair, wrapped her other arm around his neck, and braced herself for—

A sharp pinch. A flood of delight. The sensation of Kalen drinking.

Fawn squeezed her eyes shut at the startling pleasure. She barely realized how tight her fingers fisted in his hair, or how hard her fingers dug into his shoulder until he growled. His arms came around her in a fierce embrace, lifting her feet from the floor.

A moan fled her lips.

Sweet gods. She'd made a mistake. A fatal mistake to her heart.

She felt his mouth leave her neck an instant before it crushed down on her lips. His kiss was brutally delicious, desperate, demanding, and vulnerable. He breathed life into her soul, fanned the sparks of promise and rightness, sowing the visions of a happily ever after.

Kalen's head jerked back and he placed her on her feet. He glanced at the door before slowly licking the corners of his mouth. Fawn watched the flick of his tongue, captivated. Clumsily, she made an effort to compose herself and wipe a hint of blood from his chin. The tenderness in his gaze when he looked down at her made butterflies swirl in her belly.

The door opened and Jackson poked his head in. "I think we should go."

Kalen sighed. Fawn pressed her lips together, her cheeks warming.

"I'll be right there," Kalen said.

Jackson nodded. "Fawn, I left a number in that bag. It's to a disposable phone. If you need anything, call me on that number. I'll be back in town by morning to welcome Mr. Mad Scientist."

Jackson left.

"Kalen." Fawn swallowed down the small knot in her throat. "I know this is going to be asking the world of you, but..."

Kalen touched the tip of his finger to her bottom lip. "I trust you."

Her heart fluttered. How he knew she was about to ask him to do exactly that, she hadn't a clue. There was no hesitation in his declaration.

Kalen dipped his head, mouth brushing her ear. "Thank you, Faunalyn. You've stolen a piece of my heart."

Like a ghost, he was gone before she had time to react to his confession. She lunged for the open door and watched Jackson pop his car into a U-turn and drive away.

Never in her life had she thought of her home as cold and desolate. Never had she believed her gardens wouldn't soothe her or provide comfort. As the fiery colors of dusk faded into midnight blue dotted with the first twinkling stars, she felt as if all the joy she found in life was sucked out of her as the red of Jackson's taillights faded into the distance.

For hours, Fawn sat at her table, staring at the rose in the vase. She couldn't shake the hollowness that took up residence in her heart. It made no sense, yet perfect sense. All of it. She wasn't about to question the possibility of love at first sight. She'd seen it happen. It was not impossible, just improbable.

She'd initially been struck by Kalen's amazing looks, but it was the discovery of a complex soul struck with both innocence and wisdom hard-earned through his experiences that hooked her by the heartstrings.

At last, Fawn got up and put a pot of water on the stove. She pulled out a tin of dried flowers and herbs, scooped a serving with a metal steeper, and dropped it into the bottom of a mug. Maybe after a good solid sleep, she'd think more clearly.

"Might as well look things over."

Fawn grabbed the bag Jackson had entrusted to her and unzipped one of the compartments to see several notebooks with handwritten notes, formulas, and results-filled pages. Typed notes were folded and stuffed within the pages. USBs were at the bottom of the compartment in a small plastic case. Each one had a sticker on it with what she presumed was a year. Five total. Many more years were somewhere within this bag. Years of mysteries to be unraveled.

The main section of the bag held Jackson's laptop, along with pieces of equipment she couldn't begin to figure out. Boxes and bags and containers and things she didn't even recognize.

She'd figure this stuff out. Kalen and Vivian's lives depended on it.

She located the paper with the mobile number and put the information in her cell phone. As she closed the bag and prepared to tuck it in her bedroom, she felt another square object on a side she hadn't opened. She would have passed it off as another box with some scientific something or other had her fingers not warmed with unexplained energy.

"What on earth?"

Fawn tugged open the zipper and pulled out a plain white box. Square in shape with a sticker from Delaney's Delectables on the front.

"I don't recall your delectables possessing magical energy, Delaney," she murmured, sliding the cover off the box. "Holy goddess."

The top slipped from her weak fingers.

Fawn rubbed her eyes, making sure she wasn't seeing things. If that was…if what she was looking at was…

With trembling hands, she lifted the delicate circlet from the box and stared at the intricate gold work inlaid with clear stones. An oblong moonstone glowed from the front of the ancient fae crown. Its power pulsed through Fawn's fingers and up her arms like a soft breath.

"Why is this in Jackson's bag?" she murmured, hoping an answer would come to her from thin air. At this point, she didn't care if spirits spoke to her. She needed to find out who this belonged to, why Jackson had it, and what it meant for Kalen and Vivian.

And there was only one person she knew who could answer the questions rolling through her head.

Fawn quickly pulled up her contacts and dialed.

"Hi, Fawn—"

"Willa, I need to see you. It's urgent."

Willa Iscove, owner of Illusions, and Lapidus fae. She knew her stones and metals. If anyone could give her an answer, it was Willa.

"Yes, of course. I'm just finishing up with a piece at the store. Where are you?"

"Home. I'll come by, if that's okay."

"Sure. I'll leave the back door unlocked. Come in when you get here."

Chapter 10

"My brother."

Kalen caught his sister's reflection in the window as she silently stepped up behind him. Her small arms circled his waist and her cheek pressed against his back. Kalen stared out into the forest surrounding the isolated cabin. Clouds crept across the sky, dampening the glow of the moon and obscuring the stars. Nocturnal wildlife skittered through the trees. Every few minutes, Kalen caught the flash of eyes or a shadow of movement.

His mind wasn't focused on his surroundings tonight.

Faunalyn filled him. Her warm golden life essence hummed through his veins and consumed his mind with the raw desire to make her his. He had no right to think such things, not when his life was not his own. She gave him a reason to fight for himself and not solely for Vivian.

He wanted Faunalyn. He wanted to learn the world by her side. Learn how to love and be loved.

Kalen rested his hands over Vivian's and sighed. "You should be resting to keep your strength."

"Whether I walk around or lie down will not determine how long my strength remains. It's when Faunalyn's magic wears off that determines the will of my strength to fade, because I can't defeat the monster inside me."

"Yes, Vivi. You can. You will. I won't let you succumb."

Her arms tightened in a loving squeeze. She released him and shifted to stand by his side. Kalen draped an arm around her shoulders.

"Look at us, Kalen. Fugitives. Innocent fugitives."

"But we're free of the lab."

"We're not *free*, though." Vivian nuzzled her cheek into his side. "You drank from her."

Kalen stiffened. A storm of emotion came over him at his sister's knowledge. He'd never fed directly from a source, and Vivian knew it. She also knew his determination *not* to feed from any living creature.

"She's special, Kalen. I see what she does to you. There's an ease about you that wasn't there before. She makes you happy."

"How do you know this?"

Vivian grinned when she looked up at him. It was a relief to see his beautiful sister in those eyes and that expression, not the beast that ate her away day by day.

"I'm a woman, too. I may not have the experience most have, but I suspect I understand the look in your eyes when you look at her. A similar look in her eyes when she sees you. The energy between you two is undeniable." Vivian tapped a finger on his chest before turning back to the window. "Nicholas told us both about the light in the soul. Does she bring light to your soul, Kalen?"

Kalen's lips curled into a grin. He couldn't help it. Thoughts about Faunalyn and that golden glow provided him a sense of security and perfection.

He nodded. "I believe so. But how am I to know another won't do the same?"

"There is so little I remember of Momma, but one thing always stuck close. She told me once, before we were captured, that when we meet the one we're meant to be with, we can see the universe in their eyes during the full moon. I don't know why or how I've remembered that, since I was so young when we lost her, but I have. I can almost hear her voice when I recall the memory." Vivian pointed to the cloudy sky. "A full moon draws near. Perhaps you should see if there is truth behind our mother's claim."

"Sounds more like a myth than a truth." Although he wouldn't mind putting it to the test. "Poetic romance."

"A sliver of hope." Her palm rested over his heart. "I do not want to be the one who destroys you, brother. My heart would not survive. But it is your vow to protect me that created the gallant man you have become. Don't throw her away because of me."

"Oh, Vivi." Kalen kissed the top of her head. "We'll get through this. We'll come out the victors in the end. I will not give you up, my sister."

"Then promise me you will not give her up, either."

The words were easy to form, but the weight of the promise pressed down on his shoulders. Guilt that someone who meant just as much to him as his sister had slipped into his life.

"I promise."

"Thank you, Kalen." Vivian yawned. "I think I'm going to watch some television. I should give Jackson a reason to believe I still have some control over myself."

Despite Vivian's soft laughter as she left the room, he felt no humor in her words. Tonight, she had control. Tomorrow, she *might* have that control. But what would happen in another day or two when the magic wore off and the feral vampire took over? Without Faunalyn's help, Vivian would continue her downward spiral until she became the monster Dr. Hamstead portrayed her as.

We will find a cure, Kalen. I did not plan this escape for nothing. You and Vivian deserve a life, and I'll be damned if I can't give you a chance to live. Our time is short, though. The enhanced DNA is replicating at a greater speed than your normal DNA. It's working to destroy the foundation of your sister's person. If that happens, be prepared. There will be no other option but to end her life.

That had been the last conversation Kalen had with Nicholas before the ambush. Vivian had been sedated while Nicholas confided in Kalen the brutal truth of their situation. Promise lay in Nocturne Falls, but in reality, nothing was promised to him or Vivian. He refused to believe he'd lose his sister.

Yet he couldn't help but face the very real possibility Vivian would not survive for a chance at life.

"If there's a problem with Delaney's treats, she might be the person you need to see."

Fawn snorted, resting the flat square box on the table in front of Willa. "This is beyond chocolate, Willa. I don't think Delaney keeps anything like this in her back room at the shop." She slid the top off and pushed the box closer to her friend. Willa looked at the circlet, her honey blond hair falling over her cheeks. Her forehead creased as she reached in and lifted out the ancient fae crown.

Willa's eyes widened slowly, the aquamarine glinting with a mixture of awe and concern. "Where did you get this?"

"Do you know what it is? Where it's from? Can you tell me *anything* about this?"

"It's fae."

"That much I *do* know." Fawn pulled up a stool and sat beside Willa. The fae woman turned the circlet in her hands, bringing it closer to her face as she inspected its detailed craftsmanship of interlaced gold. "The energy coming off it screams fae. But…what species?"

"I've never seen one of these, only heard of them through stories and books." Willa glanced up at her window. "Come with me."

"Where?"

Willa hopped off her chair and wove through her workbenches to the window. Fawn hurried to catch up.

"You're right about the energy. It's strong, but that doesn't mean this is a direct correlation to the species I'm thinking. There's only one way to find out for sure."

Willa twisted the circlet so the moonstone angled toward the window. The moonlight cut through the clouds and bathed the stone in silvery light.

The resulting display against the wall drew a gasp from Fawn's throat.

Thousands of tiny twinkling dots shimmered over the wall. Spirals blended into those dots, creating a stunning image of a piece of the universe.

"Wow," Willa murmured. "Where did you say you got this?"

"I found it tucked in a bag given to me." Fawn touched the wall. The dots glowed against the back of her hand. "What is this?"

"The universe." Willa turned away from the window as the clouds slipped in front of the moon and the spectacular image faded from the wall. Her brows rose when her gaze met Fawn's. "This belongs to a Celestial fae. A royal. How did you end up with it?" Willa's gaze flicked toward her table. "In one of Delaney's boxes?"

Fawn chewed her lower lip, holding out a hand for the circlet. She knew she could trust Willa, and right now, she needed someone with more knowledge about fae than she had to help her decipher this.

"You don't know what you have here, do you? The significance of this?" Willa asked. Fawn shook her head. "Celestial fae are believed to be more spiritual beings than flesh and blood. Some believe they're deities. Others believe they're lore. They're overseers of the universe and knowledge wielders of the stars. Few have seen them, and those who have called them angelic in appearance with star-studded eyes."

Well, that certainly described Kalen and Vivian.

Fawn tried to keep her heart from beating out of her chest as Willa's excitement grew. She had yet to relinquish the circlet to Fawn.

"So, you're telling me that belongs to a royal Celestial fae?" Fawn asked.

Willa shrugged. "It sure looks that way. But they don't separate from their crowns willingly. My understanding of Celestial fae is that their powers come from the stone, and increase during the waxing phase of the moon when on Earth. Moonlight gives them a ghostly appearance, less corporeal."

Kalen certainly had a ghostly appearance, but she'd blamed that on his lack of blood. Now, she wondered how much of his paleness was because he might be Celestial fae.

Was it possible he was of royal fae blood?

The prospect excited and saddened her. If he was royal, there could be no hope for anything between them. She was an elf, not pure fae. He might not be pure fae, but he had royalty in his veins, something she knew nothing about.

"Fawn, what's going on?" Willa asked, her voice lowering and genuine concern seeping in. She held out the circlet and Fawn took it with a sigh. Willa rested a hand on her shoulder. "Something's eating at you."

"Yes." She traced one of the gold curls with her thumb, then met Willa's gaze. "I think I know who this belongs to, and they're in trouble."

Chapter 11

Two days after Kalen left, Jackson paid Fawn a visit at Magical Mayhem to give her a heads up that Dr. Hamstead was in town, and he'd brought an entourage. Jackson had been visited by the maniacal doctor, and Fawn didn't doubt she'd be on his list of people to see in the near future. She wanted to talk to Jackson about the circlet, especially now that Willa confirmed its authenticity after inspecting an ancient tome with sketches of Celestial fae.

She hadn't told Willa about Kalen and Vivian, although she was beginning to believe she might need to bring her friend into the loop. Willa possessed knowledge Fawn didn't have, and Kalen would need.

"You know, Fawn, if you were any more preoccupied, you might poof away to wherever your mind is."

Fawn glanced up from her desk, closing the notebook she had been reading. Wendy's narrowed eyes met Fawn's.

"Wanna talk about it?"

Fawn sighed and shook her head. "There's nothing to talk about." She tucked the book into her bag and locked her bag in her bottom drawer. She'd never used the lock before today. "If it's slowing down out front, you can leave for the day."

"Actually, there's a man in front who's asking for you by name." The corner of Wendy's mouth scrunched up and she squinted. "I've never seen him before, but I wouldn't trust him. There's a...scent, if you will."

Fawn's heart sputtered. Her stomach flipped as she stood up. "Did he give you a name?"

Wendy shook her head.

There was no doubt who stood in her shop, asking for her.

Shaking the turmoil from her mind, she straightened her shoulders and left her office.

A tall, rather handsome man in his sixties peered through the glass cases at her display of fruit and granola mixtures. He was impeccably dressed in a suit, sans tie, his salt-and-pepper hair neatly combed back from a tanned face creased with fine lines.

"May I suggest a smoothie?" Fawn asked, trying to get a solid read on the guy. He caught her gaze through the glass. Dark eyes, as dark as night, did a slow sweep over her as he straightened to his full height. Not impressively tall like Kalen, but certainly a few solid inches over her. His height didn't matter, though. The air of authority that thrummed around him was enough to compensate for those lacking inches. "I also have fruit and granola bowls, if that interests you."

"Actually,"—the man's voice purred with power, setting her on edge—"I was hoping to speak with Faunalyn Ayre."

"You're looking at her." Fawn gave him a smile, fake as it may be. She didn't offer her hand. She couldn't get a good gauge on the man. His vibe was certainly off, as Wendy warned. He appeared human, but something in those eyes spoke otherwise. "And who are you?"

"My name is Gerald Hamstead. I'm here following a lead in a murder investigation. The sheriff gave me your name."

Fawn's smile grew tight.

"Are you law enforcement? I haven't heard of a murder around here. Do you have credentials?"

Gerald Hamstead, slippery leech, pulled out a bifold wallet and flashed her a badge that looked very real. The card that accompanied it looked like the FBI ID she'd seen on TV shows and movies. Fawn's eyes narrowed. She'd have to ask Jackson about the doctor and whether he was, in fact, part of the government agency.

She leaned close to the wallet and confirmed the name. She lifted her attention to his face, her curiosity genuine. So was the faint chill that seeped from her spine to slither down her back. "What can I do for you?"

"I was informed that an accident occurred on your property about a week ago. Did you witness the accident?"

Dear gods, his gaze pierced her like scalding picks. He made her itch in her skin. Her own magic recognized the threat, the danger, and stirred up to shield her.

Fawn shook her head, keeping to the story she'd told Alex and Hank. "No. I was questioned about it by our local sheriff's office. I'll tell you exactly what I told them. I was unaware of an accident occurring that night. No one came through my yard or knocked on my door. Had the deputy who questioned me not come by, I would never have known there was an accident."

Gerald's eyes flashed, and his eyelids lowered slightly. Enough to warn her he didn't believe her. His smile was anything but friendly.

He nodded once as he reached into a pocket inside his jacket. He unfolded a photo and held it up for her to see. Fawn had to swallow back the lump in her throat and the sudden rush of warmth that threatened to give her away with a fierce flush to the cheeks.

The moment she saw the photograph, she knew she was in trouble. If he showed it to her, he'd most certainly showed it to Hank, which meant this monster knew she was connected to Kalen and Vivian.

"This is a picture of the suspects. Have you seen them?" Gerald asked, his gaze hardening.

Fawn shrugged and shook her head. "I may have seen the man in here, but I can't be certain."

"If that guy came in here, you'd have remembered. So would I," Wendy said, coming up beside Fawn. "Wow. Pity he's a suspect. He's by far one of the hottest men I've seen."

Fawn snickered and elbowed Wendy in the side. "Don't let your boyfriend hear you talk like that."

Wendy's hands flew up. "Hey, I said 'one.' Not 'the.' I'm safe. Is that his girlfriend?"

"They are a brother-sister team believed to have brutally murdered a man in Tennessee and stolen his car," Gerald said, his gaze hardening on Fawn. "*Brutally* murdered, Ms. Ayre. It's only a matter of time before they strike again. We need to get them off the street, and fast, so I'd suggest that if you know anything, you tell me."

Fawn straightened, her back stiffening. Her cordiality fled and she met the man's gaze with a cold one of her own. "As I said, Mr. Hamstead, I am not familiar with either one of those people. I have no knowledge of the accident. I'm sorry I can't help you."

"You are aware that by withholding information, you can be arrested and charged—"

Fawn cut him off with a sharp wave of her hand. "Don't go flaunting the threats. I'm aware of the law and what can happen. I have nothing to hide."

Oh, you've everything to hide.

"Then can you explain how you were seen with this man at a bar the other night?"

Wendy released a sharp breath.

Fawn snorted. "Easy. Someone saw wrong."

"You're telling me that the owner of the bar incorrectly identified this man as being a friend of yours from out of town?" Skepticism filled every note of his voice, flooding her with ice and anger.

She braced her hands on the counter and challenged Hamstead. "What I'm saying is that I do not know the two people in that photo. What someone tells you is between you and that person. I'm telling you that the man and woman in that photo"—Fawn flicked the flimsy paper with her finger—"are unknown to me."

She pushed off the counter, letting a warm spill of power calm her buzzing nerves.

"Now, if you'll excuse me, I have work that I must see to. If you have any further questions, I'd suggest you bring Sheriff Merrow along for the ride."

Hamstead folded the photo and tucked it back inside his jacket. He nodded once, his gaze lingering on her a moment longer, then turned and left the store. She stood behind the counter and watched through the front window long enough to see two suited men meet Hamstead in front of a black SUV.

"Damn it." Fawn's fingers fisted by her sides as she waited until the SUV pulled away from the curb. She ignored the two customers who came in a moment later, spinning to return to the back of the shop. Wendy told the customers she'd be right back, then followed on Fawn's heels as she stormed into the office. She trembled with anxiety and adrenaline. Her heart beat wildly in her chest, leaving her lightheaded. "Damn!"

"Fawn, what's going on? What's—"

She jerked around to Wendy, grabbed her shoulders and hissed, "Stay here and hold down the store. Got it?"

Wendy's eyes widened and she nodded. "But—"

"Don't answer any questions for anyone." Fawn unlocked her drawer, grabbed her purse, and pushed past Wendy. "I'll be right back."

She dug out her cell phone as she hurried across the parking lot to her car. By the time she dropped into the seat behind the wheel—after a scan of her surroundings to make sure she wasn't being followed—she activated the call. Jackson answered almost immediately.

"So? How'd your meeting—"

"Your doctor is an FBI agent?" Fawn popped the car into reverse. Tires squealed as she slammed on the gas. "Think you might've told me that?"

"Fawn, he's not an FBI agent. He's imitating an agent."

"Then why hasn't he been reported? I can only imagine the FBI takes it pretty seriously when someone pretends to be an agent, complete with fake ID. That might stop all of this." She jerked the wheel, smacked the shifter into Drive, and peeled out of the lot. One eye on her rearview mirror, she headed straight to the sheriff's office. "I can't believe this. The guy knows I've been with Kalen."

"Well, that's not good."

"No kidding!"

"Fawn, calm down. How did he—"

"Bridget told him! Kalen came into Howler's and I introduced him as a friend. How the heck am I supposed to get out of that one? There's only so much denial to go around before my lie is exposed. If this doctor interviews Hank and he confirms his sister's story…" Fawn groaned, smacking a hand against the wheel. "Hey, before I try and fix this, want to fill me in on the crown you left in the bag?"

Jackson cleared his throat. She pictured him fidgeting. "Oh, about that."

"Yeah, about that. You know, if you're going to leave me little bits and pieces of paranormal goodies, you should give me a heads up. Does that belong to Kalen?"

"That belonged to his mother."

Fawn almost ran a stop sign in her anger. She jammed on her brakes, earned the honk of a horn as a car swerved to miss her front end, and waited a moment before speeding ahead.

"They're of royal blood, Jackson. Did you know that?"

"Well, I might have had a suspicion."

"Jackson! They don't know what species of fae they are and you do? And you haven't told them? Dear goddess of Earth! What else do you know?"

"A bit."

"Guess what, Mr. Know-It-All. You'd better get in your car and meet me at the sheriff's office. We're having a long talk with Hank and we're going to put an end to this before Mr. Hyde shoves his nose deeper into this town."

Birdie perked up when Fawn stormed into the sheriff's office. Her smile never faltered as her brows rose. "Why, hello, Fawn. Did you want to speak with Hank?"

"You betchya. Need to talk to him now."

Fawn wasn't one to disrespect law enforcement, or anyone for that matter, but she was enraged.

She was *scared*.

"Hi, Fawn." Hank stepped out of his office, his smile of greeting barely noticeable. His blue eyes watched her carefully. "Come on back."

Fawn hurried into Hank's office and dropped into one of the chairs in front of his desk. The sheriff closed the door and took up his seat, folding his hands over his blotter.

"Jackson is coming."

Hank's brow arched. "Jackson Emery? Care to tell me why Jackson would be coming here?"

"To set things right."

Hank leaned back in his chair and regarded her with suspicion. It was the first time she had ever earned a look from him that made her feel like a criminal.

"Listen, maybe I should've said something earlier, but I didn't. That's done. I'm going to say something now, but I need you to listen to me, *really* listen to me, and not go running to Hamstead. He paid me a visit right before I came here, claiming he's FBI."

"Excuse me?"

Fawn nodded. "He has forged credentials. He's not FBI. He's a doctor at a lab along the Canadian border. He kidnaps paranormals and experiments on them."

Jackson had better put his foot to the pedal.

A furrow deepened over the sheriff's brows. "I'm listening."

Fawn shifted in her seat, suddenly uncomfortable. She'd come here with a purpose, but now she wondered whether she could trust the werewolf watching her with quiet accusation.

"This is beyond anything we've seen in Nocturne Falls. In the time I've been here, I've never once seen you, or any of the core residents of this town, turn their back on a paranormal who needs help."

"What does that have to do with Jackson?" Hank rocked back in his chair. "And I'm beginning to suspect this is more about the *friend* paying you a visit."

"Everything."

Silence stretched. Fawn rubbed a hand over her eyes, trying to get her thoughts straight. She'd make a decision in a matter of moments, a decision that could very well ruin her in Kalen's eyes.

"Fawn?"

Fawn pulled her purse onto her lap and dug out the notebook she had been studying at her shop. She dropped it on the desk in front of Hank.

"I wasn't completely honest with you. Or Alex." She fiddled with her fingers in her lap. "I did witness the accident."

Hank became still. His brows rose subtly. She caught a flare of surprise in his expression before it vanished.

"You lied to me."

Fawn turned her gaze to the ceiling. "Yes. But I have reasons." She pointed to the notebook. "Very good reasons for not telling you. I'm telling you now because Kalen and his sister, Vivian, are in trouble, and Hamstead is the source of that trouble."

"I've never known you to lie, Fawn. What made you cover for a suspected murderer?"

A defensive flare burst to life. "He's not a murderer. And neither is his sister. I don't know all the details—that's why I told Jackson to come here to help me explain—but I know enough to tell you they would never have killed the man Hamstead claims they did."

Fawn went on to tell Hank what she knew, from Nicholas helping Kalen and Vivian escape the lab to the experiment on Vivian gone wrong. With each sentence, guilt swelled. She only hoped the man she considered one of her good friends in this town would believe her, and maybe even offer his help.

A knock on the door interrupted her as she started to go into Kalen's half-fae, half-vampire breeding.

"Come in," Hank said.

Jackson slipped into the room. He appeared as disheveled as always, hair mussed, clothing wrinkled and haphazardly put together. He rubbed the back of his neck as he took the empty chair beside Fawn, flashed her a timid grin, and began fidgeting in his seat.

"Fawn's been filling me in on this problem we seem to have." The sheriff tapped the notebook. He hadn't touched it until now, although his attention continually drifted over the worn cover. "So, Jackson, I understand you have some secrets, too."

"Sheriff, sir, I can explain," Jackson said, his voice cracking.

"Explain to me, then, why you're housing the suspects in your uncle's murder."

Jackson shot Fawn a helpless look. "They didn't kill my uncle. If I were to guess, Dr. Hamstead ordered him killed after he helped Kalen and Vivian escape his facility. My uncle was the only scientist at the lab they could trust. Uncle Nick had worked for Hamstead when their parents were in captivity. He helped in their escape before resigning. Hamstead asked him to come back about three years after Kalen and Vivian were captured. I'm still going through the notes and data my uncle sent me, but there are hints Dr. Hamstead is responsible for the deaths of Kalen and Vivian's parents after their escape from the lab. You see, their parents were used as an experiment to see if it was possible to create a vampire without the UV allergy."

"Wait, what?" Hank leaned forward heavily on his desk, his eyes narrowed. This was not the side of the interrogation Fawn cared to be on. "I'm not sure I'm getting you."

"Uh, well..." Jackson cleared his throat and adjusted his glasses for the third time. He caught Fawn's eyes. "Did you tell him what they are?"

Fawn shook her head. "I was about to when you got here."

"What who are?" Hank interrupted.

Fawn sighed. "Kalen and Vivian are half-fae, half-vampire. They can walk in the sun, unlike most vampires, and retain their fae-like traits."

"Vampires producing offspring with anything other than another vampire is practically unheard of."

"Their mother was Celestial fae, which I think might have been a loophole in the offspring problem. The Celestials are a different composition than most fae, and their power is ancient enough to balance the power of a vampire. Really, it's a perfect match, if you're looking for a new breed of powerful species." Jackson crossed and uncrossed his legs. "Dr. Hamstead has been studying the paranormal for quite some time, according to my uncle. He's obsessed with immortality, but won't allow himself to be changed until he knows he won't have to give up the sunlight. He wants power, strength, and all the trimmings without any restrictions or repercussions, such as the craze that can potentially consume a newly turned neck-biter. He's been experimenting with Kalen and Vivian since they were children, trying to develop the perfect DNA structure that would give him all the benefits of immortality and strength and none of the drawbacks. Unfortunately, the last experiment he performed on Vivian went wrong and it's turning the vampire in her genetic coding on the fae part of."

Hank shook his head, his expression one of disbelief and confusion. Fawn had never seen the man look so lost. She didn't blame him. All the talk of genetic coding and DNA structure was a different language to her, too.

"In a nutshell for those of us who aren't geniuses in the scientific field, the last experiment has turned Vivian's own body against her. She's turning more crazed vampire than controlled fae. Nicholas staged the escape after Hamstead ordered Vivian to be put down."

Hank dragged a hand down his mouth and chin. His head dropped as he opened the notebook. "This sounds a bit far-fetched."

"Sir, I understand—"

The sheriff cut Jackson off. "But I've seen lots of far-fetched things in this town. Fawn." He glanced up at her quickly. "Don't you ever lie to me again, got it?"

Fawn nodded, her cheeks warming. "I'm so sorry. If I'd asked for help instead of lying, we might've been able to thwart the doctor's attempt to find them. Which reminds me. Bridget told Hamstead or his men about me bringing Kalen to Howler's. They know I've had contact with him, though I denied it."

"Let me get this straight. Dr. Hamstead is posing as an FBI agent who is trying to find Kalen and his sister to return them to a lab for experimental purposes? He's trying to create a new vampire breed?" Hank ran through a few more details of what she and Jackson had told him. Listening to their story from his mouth sounded about as far-fetched as he proposed, but in the end, Hank nodded. "Where are Kalen and Vivian now?"

"I hid them outside Nocturne Falls," Jackson said.

"Let me get with the Ellinghams about this situation. In the meantime, keep them out of town until I give you the go-ahead to bring them back. Fawn, don't go out alone. And make sure you lock up your house at night. I'll have deputies patrol around your shop and house, but I don't have the manpower to put a deputy on you twenty-four-seven. Don't talk to Hamstead unless I'm with you, or with him. Got it?" Hank handed the notebook back to Fawn. "I'll want to see that again, and whatever evidence you have supporting Kalen and Vivian's case. For now, keep it safe. I'm going to try and locate Hamstead and question him about his credentials."

Fawn packed the notebook away and stood up as Hank came around the desk. Jackson scrambled to his feet and followed Fawn into the lobby.

"Birdie, if anyone needs me, you know how to reach me. I'll be back later," Hank said as they left the department. Fawn paused on the sidewalk. Jackson rocked back to avoid walking into her. The sheriff gave her shoulder a gentle squeeze. "Stay around people until I get the patrol set up, okay? And you have my cell number if there's an emergency."

"Of course. Thanks, Hank."

Fawn waited until Hank got into his police cruiser before she turned to Jackson. "Today's your lucky day, Jackson. I'm going to teach you how to make smoothies with a dash of mayhem."

Chapter 12

"Any news?"

Kalen followed at Jackson's heels, anxious to learn about the happenings in Nocturne Falls. By some power of gods and goddesses and spirits alike, Vivian had maintained control over the monster for four days. It wasn't until a little while ago that Kalen noted the subtle changes in her demeanor that warned the magic was wearing off—the blank stares, the rigid posture, and the tic at the corner of her mouth.

Time was borrowed, as he'd heard many Lab Coats say. Vivian had borrowed far more time than she should ever have had access to.

"Dr. Hamstead has been elusive. Sheriff Merrow is trying to locate him with the help of the Ellinghams. They think he and his men may be staying outside the town limits."

"I still don't like it that you told the sheriff about me and Vivian," Kalen groused.

"I kind of had my hands tied, Kal. We've been through this. Quite a number of times, actually. Fawn had revealed too much."

The mention of Faunalyn ignited the heat and desire he suffered at the very sound of her name. When Jackson confided what he and Fawn had done—revealing his situation to the sheriff—he had been enraged. He had trusted Faunalyn with his secrets, with Vivian's secrets, and she had betrayed him.

Two days later, it still stung, but his longing to see her, to make sure she was safe, edged past that hurt. Her safety had begun to take priority.

Jackson rubbed his hands over his face and sank into a chair at the kitchen table. The man looked ten times more worn and ruffled than usual, his eyes red-rimmed in the hollows of dark circles. Kalen was ever grateful the man, going on sheer trust from his uncle, worked endlessly to try and help them.

"You know, Kalen, she made a very valid point the night we left Nocturne Falls. I've lived there for years, but never really integrated with the residents. She embraced the town, and the people, and she knows a thing or two I don't. That's why she told Sheriff Merrow. He has the connections to help you. And right now, we need every connection we can get."

"How much longer do you suppose Vivian and I will be trapped here?" Kalen asked, settling stiffly in a chair across from Jackson. It dawned on him shortly after coming to the cabin that they were in a similar situation as they had been at the lab. Trapped. Imprisoned. Only this time, they had the option of leaving if they wanted to.

Jackson's shoulders slumped. Not a promising sign. "I don't know. Fawn has been in touch with the sheriff daily. We're waiting for Hamstead to make an appearance. Once he's in custody—forging federal documentation is a very bad thing, you know—hopefully I can get you back to Nocturne Falls. In the meantime, I'm coming along with a promising antidote to Vivian's illness. It'll be a temporary fix, but it'll help. I just need a little more time."

Kalen glanced toward Vivian's room. "I'm not sure we have much time. Vivian's starting to regress again."

Jackson frowned. The sorrow in his expression piqued Kalen's interest at the same time it drew on his own manifesting grief. If Vivian lost herself to the vampire, he'd have to end her. He couldn't bear the thought, even though he and Vivi had numerous conversations about it since arriving at the cabin.

Vivian accepted her fate. Kalen cursed it.

"I should get back to work. I'll take a sweet vacation once she's cured. I'll teach you how to make pina coladas so you can serve them to me in my backyard for a month."

The rumpled man groaned as he stood up and trudged out of the kitchen. Kalen understood that hunched-shoulder, weight-of-the-universe stance. He suffered that same burden. The burden of another's life weighed precariously on the decisions he made, the developments of a cure to come, and the choices he placed in the hands of two people.

He wasn't alone long before Vivian slipped into the kitchen, fluid and ethereal in her approach. The moon, a full silvery orb in the dark sky beyond the window, made her pale hair shimmer and her skin glow. Her eyes intensified in color, the streaks of silver in her startling blue capturing the moon's brilliance.

His heart ached to see his beautiful sister and know an end drew near, all the good in her being destroyed by one man's greed.

"Are you still mad, Kalen?" she asked in the language of their mother, her voice soft. She rounded the chair closest to him and sat down, reaching for his hands. "Because you shouldn't be."

"Perhaps disappointed is a better word." He caressed Vivian's knuckles with his thumbs. "How are you feeling, Vivi?"

His sister grinned sadly. "As you said, I'm beginning to regress. But I find comfort in the moonlight. I can't explain it. The light is soothing to me. We've never seen a full moon. This is our first and the energy is outstanding. I can't describe it. I feel…lighter."

Unfortunately, Kalen had been too preoccupied to take notice of the energy from the moon. "I'm glad to hear that. Maybe it'll keep the vampire at bay."

"Maybe." She leaned closer to him, her eyes flashing. "But it's also the time to test Momma's theory."

Kalen arched a brow. "Now is not the time to chase after lore."

"Who said you'd be chasing lore, and lore alone? Surely there is more you wish to chase that doesn't involve cures and curses?"

He shook his head in defiance. "Not at this time."

"Ah, you *are* still mad." She chuckled, the sweetness of the sound ingrained in his memory. "Silly man. If anyone should be mad, it should be me. After all, I'm the one who would have murdered Nicholas, right? A monster vampire with little self-control. Hamstead painted a picture worthy of believing. But I'm not angry because I believe what Faunalyn did will help us. You. I believe she did it with our best interest in mind."

Vivian dipped her head and kissed the back of his hand before she pressed her cheek to his knuckles. For a long while, they stayed like that, her head on his hands, the moonlight pouring over her hair. She gave him time to pick through his emotions, so many emotions that were new to him.

At last, she climbed to her feet and kissed the top of his head. "I know, dear brother, you feel the same way as I. So, go to her tonight. I'll be fine until you return."

Kalen sat alone at the table for what seemed like a short eternity after Vivian took her leave, trying to make sense of what swelled inside his chest and the pain deeper in his soul. If movies and television shows were correct, then he had a good idea what these strange sensations meant.

They meant something he never expected to experience, nor wanted to experience. Not now, at least, because it diverted his attention from his sister's welfare.

Fate had a different idea, it seemed, because Fate gave him an ultimatum.

Now…or never.

A scratch drew Fawn's attention from the book on her desk and toward her bedroom door. Her heart fluttered into a quickened pace, and her breath choked her. Since Hamstead's visit at her shop, she'd been on edge. Every noise, every unexpected breeze, every unusual nuance put her on hyper alert. She was treading paranoia, all because she felt the doctor's presence nearby. She had yet to catch him or his men watching her, but her gut warned her not to let her guard down.

The breeze had kicked up to a low gusting wind. Branches scraped along her windows and the siding of her house. She dismissed the noise after a few minutes of familiar sounds and went back to reading up on Celestial fae. The book belonged to Willa's family. It had been collecting dust in her homeland. Documentation on Celestial fae was rare, and from the uncertainty in the notes of this particular hand-written book, Fawn didn't doubt that.

A scratch and a bump jerked her straight in her chair.

Fawn quietly got to her feet and started out of her bedroom. She kept a small nightlight on in the kitchen. The only other light in the house came from her desk lamp. Her curtains were drawn, only a dappling of silvery glow coming through the thick, gauzy material.

A shadow moved across the floor in the moonlight cast through one of the narrow windows flanking her front door.

Fawn drew back. She ducked to hide behind the kitchen counter. A knock cut through the dense silence.

"Fawn, it's Hank."

A heavy sigh fled her lips as she straightened up and hurried to the front door. Sure enough, Hank waited on her front stoop, scanning the forest behind him.

"Come in." Fawn stepped to the side to let the sheriff in and closed the door behind him. "Sorry. I've been jumpy."

"I still don't understand why you haven't stayed with someone closer to town until we get this figured out." Hank hooked his thumbs on his duty belt as he turned to face her. "We've got a suspected location of Dr. Hamstead in a neighboring city. That city police department is looking into the lead."

"Thank the gods." Fawn rested a hand against her chest. "Have you told Jackson?"

"Not yet. I wanted to drop by, do a perimeter check until I get another patrol out here, and give you the news."

"Thanks. And thank Hugh again for the blood supply. I should see Jackson tomorrow to get it to Kalen."

"I'll be sure to pass that along. Hugh wants to meet the brother-sister duo. He might be able to help with finding a cure. He's got a thing for chemistry and probably has equipment Jackson doesn't."

Fawn managed a smile, though her thoughts went to Vivian and how the woman might be holding up—or not. She didn't know Hugh well other than as Delaney's husband and one of the town leaders, but she'd give anything and anyone who could help save Vivian a chance. It might not be her place to make that decision, but she knew the people of Nocturne Falls and their willingness to come together for each other.

"That would be wonderful. I just hope we catch Hamstead before Vivian is too far gone."

Hank nodded once and gave Fawn's shoulder a squeeze. A chill flicked along the nape of her neck, but disappeared as soon as it came. She chalked it up to nerves.

"We'll get him. I promise you that. No one comes into my town, impersonates a federal agent, threatens my friends, and stays out of my line of sight for long. Hang tight, Fawn. It's only a matter of time now."

Fawn watched Hank stride down the dirt path to his cruiser before she closed the door, locked up, and headed back to her room. She stifled a yawn, rubbed her eyes, and sighed. She really needed to get some sleep.

"Why did you tell him?"

The shriek that fled her lips could have broken glass. She flew back, stumbling as her legs gave way beneath the fright. Hands, firm but tender, grabbed her arms and steadied her on her feet before she had a chance to fall flat on her butt.

Her gaze crashed into Kalen's.

Oh dear, sweet goddess almighty.

She'd be lying if she said the sight of him didn't melt her where she stood. His scent, clean and pure, washed away the anxiety of the last four days. He awoke the magic inside her soul until she felt the warm glow consume her veins.

But Kalen looked different.

He looked like an ethereal creation of mind and magic, imagination and wistful thinking. A shimmer of moonlight seeped into her room through the curtains, and it was enough to confirm the suspicions she held since her meeting with Willa.

Kalen Hawkins was certainly Celestial fae, from the beautiful glow of his skin to the magnificent color of his eyes.

Her lips moved to answer him, but her mind couldn't think of the words she needed. All she could focus on was the fact Kalen was back, in her home.

He shifted his weight, angling her toward the window without taking his hands from her arms. "Why did you tell him my secrets? I trusted you."

Fawn licked her lips. Her mouth had gone bone dry. Shame stirred her belly in a not-so-pleasant circle, one she could very well do without at the moment.

She moved according to his direction, closer and closer to the window. One step every few moments, a slow dance in preparation of something far more explosive. The sensation was unusual, awkward, and completely alluring.

"Why?"

"I…" She cleared her throat. "You need more help than I can give you. The people of this town, my friends, those I trust, are working to protect you and your sister."

"How can you be so sure?"

He didn't appear angry. Nor did he appear saddened. His questions seemed to come out of curiosity more than a sense of betrayal. His face was relaxed, his eyes brilliantly bright and luminous as the moonlight cut across his face.

"It's something I know. Something I feel deep inside me. An understanding that those I've confided in, those who know your secret now, will do what they must to help me help you. It's instinct. Sometimes, Kalen, feelings can't be explained rationally. It's not only people we learn to trust. We must trust the subtle whispers of our subconscious, too. The one I listened to the night of your accident when I tried to help you and Vivian."

Kalen remained quiet, his gaze probing beyond her skin and deeper, into her mind. She could almost feel his energy mixing with her own, a hint of magic she believed he didn't know he possessed melding with the magic running through her veins.

"What am I, Faunalyn?"

His voice was soft, just above a whisper. A tinge of uncertainly hung on his question, a hint of desperation to understand the fundamental aspects of his own self edged his words.

Fawn reached up and cupped one side of his face. The glow of his skin from the small sliver of moonlight cast her own fingers in a silvery haze, an effect she would relate to a human trying to touch a spirit.

"You are someone truly special. Someone I will fight for until you are free."

Kalen drew back one of the curtains and lifted her chin.

His eyes narrowed after a long, drawn-out moment. "She spoke the truth."

"I don't understand. Who?"

"Vivian. The moon. I feel...different with the moon. I can't put it into words." Kalen released her chin and made a fluid motion with his fingers. Moonlight curled around his fingertips like shimmering ribbons. "We were never allowed to go outside when the moon was full. Our windows were locked shut each month. Vivi and I figured it was normal."

"Your powers are strongest during the phase of the full moon. Hamstead knew this because he knew you are Celestial fae. And not only Celestial..." Fawn lowered her hand and ducked her head as she rounded Kalen. He remained by the window, his gaze never leaving her as she reached her desk and removed the chocolate box from her bottom drawer. She worked the top off as she returned to Kalen's side. "Your mother came from a line of royals."

Whatever the future held for Kalen and herself was trivial at this point. Kalen, deprived of so much, deserved the truth. She lifted the circlet from the box and held it out to him.

"It was in the bag Jackson left with me the night he brought you to the cabin."

Kalen's brows furrowed. Slowly, he took the circlet from Fawn and brought it up to his eyes. The twining gold design deepened in color, the rich shade pulsing. Fawn blinked as the oval stone began to glow and pulse in time with the precious metal.

Tilting his head to the side, observing the object in his hands, Kalen murmured, "He knew."

"Yes. He did. Nicholas told Jackson what he knew about your mother. I found notes on a USB in the bag. It wasn't much, but it was something. I also learned what Jackson knew the day we went to see Sheriff Merrow. Dr. Hamstead came into my shop and threatened me. I've been learning much about your good doctor over the last few days, rifling through the information Jackson left with me. It's unclear whether Hamstead knew you were of royal lineage, but I doubt it. A few days before the ambush at your family's home, your mother contacted Nicholas and entrusted him with her secret. She feared that if Hamstead learned how powerful her heritage was, there would be no limit to the torture and the tests that would come."

Raw, untamed power flowed through him so strongly, it brushed her body, making her skin tingle. The magic felt hot and cold, an unusual weave of bright and dark. Like the man needed any help from magic to make him even more extraordinary. It wasn't only his impeccable looks that captivated her, but the pureness of his spirit. The innocence and determination to do what was right. This new flood of power enhanced those characteristics a hundredfold.

Fawn lowered her gaze and folded her hands in front of her. "I showed it to my friend Willa. She specializes in metals and stones. She was able to confirm what it was and who it belonged to." She nodded toward her desk. Kalen followed her gaze. "She found that book about the Celestial fae at her home and was kind enough to lend it to me. That circlet, that crown, belongs on your head. You're the oldest child of the last living royal of your house. According to the book, the royals make up a court and rule over your people. They're called the High Guard, and they oversee the universal powers that come from astral planes. Celestials seldom come to the human realm, or Earth for that matter, so there isn't a great deal of documentation available."

"If what you say is true—and I have little doubt about your words—it does not change who I am, Faunalyn. Royal blood or not, my past has made me the man I am. A man lost in this world, but one who finds hope in a few. I have not earned your submission, nor do I want it."

When Fawn lifted her gaze to Kalen, her eyes instantly went to the ethereal ropes of luminescent white that stretched from the moonstone to twine around his fingertips. Fingertips that reached for her face and touched her cheek in a tender caress.

"My mother confided something in Vivian when she was a little girl, and I'm witnessing the amazing manifestation of that small piece of our history." Kalen placed the circlet on the dresser behind her and slipped his arm around her waist. "You hold my universe in your eyes."

Fawn had no time to question his confusing words before he kissed her with full, possessive sweeps of his tongue that left her clinging to him for strength. The heat of his body encircled her, cocooned her in an embrace of pure...

No. No, it couldn't be...

But when Kalen's lips broke from hers—the damn man literally kissed the breath out of her lungs—she could not deny the emotions in his eyes. They were as plain as the color was clear.

He *loved* her.

It made her heart skip and her mind whirl. All because she understood that exact look. She *felt* it, too.

Kalen took her hand, his fingers warm and tender around hers, and brought her palm to the open V of his button-down shirt. He covered the back of her hand, splaying her fingers over the smooth skin beneath her utterly sensitive pads. Tiny bursts of heat skittered in electric spurts from fingertips to arm to that simmering desire pooling low in her belly.

"I don't want you to restrain yourself, Faunalyn. I want to know you. Every way I can. I want to know what your hands feel like as they touch my skin. I want to know the sound of your heartbeat and the pace of your breaths as you take what you want and I give what you need. I want to see the change of color in your cheeks and hear the passion in your voice." He leaned close, his cheek brushing hers as his lips teased her earlobe. She closed her eyes, desire bubbling upward, drawing more and more of her body along for the ride. "And I want you to know me in this dance called intimacy."

"Yes," she whispered.

Tonight, she would show him the full power of love.

Chapter 13

The sun had yet to breach the horizon. The light from the moon thrummed through his body, his veins, and filled each cell with magic.

The beautiful woman wrapped around his body?

He never wanted this moment to end. The absoluteness of the moment was immense.

And it didn't, for a few hours. He remained awake, listening to the steady beat of her heart as she slept. The scent of her skin and her hair teased him with every breath. The weight and warmth of her skin fed him new life.

Every now and again, he looked at the circlet on her dresser. His *crown*. To go from a prisoner, an experiment, a creature lost in this strange world to a royal of a fabled fae race was more than he wanted to take in. The status meant nothing to him. Spending his life in a small room with little freedom, he'd learned a thing or two about gratitude and appreciation. In all his time there, locked away with his sister, two innocent children at the hands of a madman, where was his *family*? Had no one thought to seek them out? Did they even know he and Vivian existed?

Had they tried to save their mother?

Sometimes, Kalen, family is but a word. Family may be nothing more than a technicality of blood and DNA. When it comes down to a defining moment, one where sacrifice is necessary, you will learn the true meaning of family. Those who stand beside you and protect you, those who fight for you, become your family.

Questions and more questions churned through him. He came to terms with the fact he may never know the answer to most of them. The more he learned about the fae in general, the lower his expectations of acceptance became. He wasn't pure-blooded. He did wonder, however, how the vampire societies would react to him. Would they shun him for his fae blood?

"Your heart beats so slowly."

Kalen lifted his head enough to look down at Faunalyn. She hadn't moved her head from his chest. He must've been so caught up in his thoughts he hadn't even realized her breathing pattern had changed.

"Enough for the fae to survive, is my understanding. Half of what I am doesn't require a beating heart. Or air in my lungs." He scooped up a handful of her hair and brought it to his nose, inhaling deeply. "I much prefer breathing."

Her soft chuckle was music to his ears. He dropped his head back on the pillow as she lifted her head and rested her chin on a fist over his chest. "I'm going to get up, shower, and make breakfast. We can watch the sun rise from the patio. It's quite spectacular most mornings, with the sunbeams cutting through the trees. I'd venture to guess it'll be your first in a very long time."

Kalen traced her delicate brow, the fine line of her cheek, the point of her ear. This woman. This wonderful, selfless woman. He couldn't begin to understand how she ended up in his life, his arms, but he thanked the gods for her.

Faunalyn placed a chaste kiss on his mouth and climbed out of bed. He didn't look away until she disappeared from the room. A few moments later, the shower started.

Kalen groaned, forcing himself from the bed and all the sweet warmth it provided. He tugged on his jeans and stepped over to the desk as he slipped his shirt onto his arms. For many minutes, he gently thumbed through the thick book left open to a page about the Celestial fae. The section on his race was small in comparison to the sections flanking it, but he began to piece together parts of who he was. Slowly, he started making sense of the behaviors of the Lab Coats around the full moon and other lunar phenomena. The sketches of his fae race were ghostly in appearance rather than solid people like him and Vivi.

He reached a page with detailed sketches of circlets, much like the one on Faunalyn's dresser. In fact, as he looked over the details of each circlet, he realized one of the sketches was *exactly* like the one Faunalyn claimed to belong to him.

"House of Xyna, Royal Court, High Guard," he read. He turned the page, hoping to learn more about the House of Xyna, only to come up empty. Seemed the book had little to offer on individual houses and bloodlines, and only a smidgen more on their magic and power.

"It's not too helpful, but it provides a little insight into your fae race."

Kalen straightened up, his attention immediately drawn to the towel-clad woman in the doorway as she ran her fingers through her wet hair. "The bloodline I belong to, I suppose, but little else. Nothing about lunar magic or how to control it. How to tap into it."

"Willa believes that your kind draws power from your circlets. The moonstone feeds your spirit power. According to her, Celestials seldom ever part with their circlets."

Bitterness seeped up the back of his throat as he cast the circlet a sharp glance. A memory of men storming the small house when he was five flooded his mind. The shrill scream from his mother as he and Vivian were torn from her sides.

He could not recall ever seeing the circlet on his mother's head. "My mother feared the circlet enough to part with it. She gave up her power, and ultimately her life."

Faunalyn's fingers stopped combing through her hair, and her arms fell to her sides. A frown dipped the corner of her mouth. "I think it's much bigger than that, Kalen, but there's so little information about your race, it's hard to say whether that circlet in the wrong hands could bring down an entire civilization. It says the High Guard oversee the astral planes, but if someone with very bad intentions can infiltrate that plane using that circlet, imagine the damage that might be inflicted on a race such as humans. You said Hamstead was trying to figure out a way to create daywalkers out of vampires. The ultimate vampire, so to speak. If he could integrate the Celestial power into one indestructible being, not only would he control what is here on Earth. He could potentially control worlds and realms."

Kalen's shoulders stiffened as Faunalyn's explanation sank in. The magnitude of what Dr. Hamstead might be trying to do made his stomach twist in a sickening knot.

In twenty-six years of tests and experiments, the doctor hadn't developed the perfect vampire, at least that Kalen was aware of. All he'd done was turn Vivian into a monster.

"I don't think he's smart enough to set such goals."

Faunalyn's brows arched and she folded her arms over her chest. "Really? Don't have to be smart to set goals. Still, if these are his goals, doesn't mean he'll reach them. He's certainly missing some nuts and bolts up here." She tapped her head. "Which makes for a frightening type of crazy. One you can't get through to because they're so wrapped up in their world."

"I need to hide the circlet."

"*We.*" Faunalyn took a step closer. The fresh scent of her floral shampoo and soap hit him, loosening his muscles from the grip of tension. "We, Kalen. I'm in this with you."

From the moment he saw what he could only describe as the universe in her eyes—a smattering of millions of stars and galaxies that went on forever—he couldn't see otherwise. The beautiful lavender-gold now held infinite possibilities and promises.

He understood her resolve, but hated the thought of putting her in danger. "I think you should dress. You're no good to me in a towel."

Faunalyn snickered. "What part of you am I no good to?"

He liked these flirtatious taunts. They were becoming easier the more time he spent with this exquisite woman. "Pick one. There are few wrong answers."

"Ah." She laughed easily, such a beautiful melody, as she brushed by him. He closed his eyes and silently prayed for the strength to keep calm. She had a way of waking him up in every possible sense of the word. "I'll be good to you this morning. Promise."

The day started as well as the night before had ended. He had never witnessed such brilliance as he watched the sun creep high into the sky, casting different hues of orange, yellow, and gold through the trees. No movie could match the real thing. He had been in complete awe until he glanced at Faunalyn and saw her watching him with no uncertain amount of adoration in her expression.

At that moment, he realized just how much he wanted to be with her. How much he adored her and…loved her.

They spent the morning on the patio. He learned much about the fierce woman, from the tension with her family over her decision to leave her small forest village to pursue a business instead of taking her place as a natural healer to her love of gardening. She had built a life in Nocturne Falls that she spoke about with pride and dignity. Her spirit was pure, her words honest and genuine, and her eyes held a deep satisfaction he only hoped he could one day know for himself.

Lunchtime rolled around and Faunalyn insisted on showing him the daytime side of Nocturne Falls. She put in a call to Jackson to get an update on Vivian—he hadn't even asked her to, although he was more concerned about his sister's welfare as the day progressed—and reassured him she was okay, after he complained to her about Kalen taking his car without asking. It put him at ease. Or maybe it was the contagious calm that seemed to roll off Faunalyn. Either way, he quickly learned the meaning of contentment, and it was a state of mind he was in no hurry to abandon.

"This town has quite a bit to take in," Kalen admitted, pausing as a streetcar passed by. Several humans packed the strange-looking vehicle, many of them children with faces pressed to the windows. As with most people he'd seen in town, the majority dressed in costumes of every kind. "For someone like me."

"It's a lot to take in for anyone who doesn't live here." She linked her arm through his and led him into another shop. This one had rows and rows of hats on oval-shaped foam heads lining the walls and some of the most interesting headwear he'd ever seen displayed on rotating metal racks throughout the main floor. "Hats in the Belfry" was painted on the wall behind the checkout counter in a magical, sparkling design. "Just to lighten the mood a bit."

Kalen was about to question her when she snagged a striped hat with a bunch of springy coils popping out every which way. She tugged it onto his head and smiled.

"There you go. Perfect disguise."

She dragged him over to a mirror and stifled a giggle behind her hand. Kalen snorted before he laughed. "Well, lovely. I think I'll blend right in with this one."

He scanned another rack until he found a suitable topper for his companion. When he pulled it off the wire arm, Faunalyn's eyes widened. "Oh no. No you don't."

"Why not? I think you can model this better than the rack." Kalen snatched her about the waist when she shuffled backward, and pulled her right up against him. Her cheeks darkened and he took advantage of her momentary lack of fight to tug the hat on. "The birds are a nice touch."

Faunalyn giggled, looking at herself in the mirror. The hat was adorned with wild nests and bird eggs, and a few small birds.

"I think my birds found some of their nesting material off your hat."

Kalen dipped his head and brushed his lips over her ear. "That might very well be the case."

"Don't you dare start that nuzzling cuteness here," she murmured. Kalen grinned to himself, recognizing the sensual strain in her voice. "You're pretty irresistible to begin with."

"Another thing we have in common, I guess." He glanced over the hats on the wall and found a pretty white brimmed hat with pale blue lilies and roses. "I think Vivi would love that."

Faunalyn took it off the display form and winked. "Then Vivi shall have it."

"Faun—"

"My gift," Faunalyn interjected before he could manage to get a full word out. The woman wove between racks, still wearing that silly bird hat, and paid for her purchase. She smiled at him as she returned to his side, linked their arms again, and led him to the door.

"Wait, we need to put these back." Kalen reached up for his hat.

"Nope. My birds need to keep their nests neat and you provide the perfect material. In other words, I bought them, too." Her soft laugh was lighthearted. Kalen groaned, his lips curling into a smile as she said, "I need to stop by my shop and get the mail."

As they emerged onto the busy sidewalk, a prickling sensation touched the back of Kalen's neck, putting him on alert. He came to a stop. Faunalyn glanced up at him.

"What is it?"

Kalen scanned the crowded streets, looking for any sign of Dr. Hamstead, or anyone else who might be watching them. He slid his arm from Faunalyn's and took off the hat. "I don't know."

No one stuck out. No one resembled any of the Lab Coats he remembered from the lab. No one appeared interested in them. Families with small children gaped and gasped and pointed at the stores and the decorations. Teenagers meandered along the sidewalks, talking about the latest trends. Every now and again, a paranormal of some sort wove through the crowd, but never caught the eye of those humans looking for real paranormals.

Such a strange, unique town.

A town that he could blend into, but also stand out in.

Right now, he felt like a glowing beacon in the dark of night. He knew he had caught the attention of an adversary hidden in the shadows.

Faunalyn's cell phone buzzed in her purse. She dug out the small, rectangular object and raised it to her ear. "Hello?"

Shamelessly, Kalen tuned in to listen to the caller.

"Hey, Fawn. It's Hank. Listen, we've got some of Hamstead's boys in custody. Found forged federal documents in their hotel rooms, plenty enough to charge them."

Kalen's eyes narrowed when Faunalyn's gaze turned up to him. A faint smile crossed her lips, but didn't reach her eyes. Apparently, she'd noticed the hesitation in the sheriff's voice, as well.

"That's good news. However, I sense a 'but' coming."

"Yeah. The 'but' is Hamstead escaped. We've impounded all three of the vehicles, so he's either moving on foot, by taxi, or rented a car under a false name. We're investigating with the city police department's help, but I wanted to give you an update."

"Thanks, Hank. I really appreciate it."

"No problem. Oh, Hugh's going to contact you later today. He wants to meet your *friend* and his sister." Hank snickered.

Kalen swallowed back a scowl as Faunalyn's cheeks flushed. Her eyes lowered and she chewed her lower lip.

"I'll be waiting for his call. Do you think he might have a solution?"

"Possibly. Keep an eye out and contact me immediately if you think you've seen Hamstead."

"You don't have to tell me twice." Faunalyn said her goodbye and slipped the phone back into her purse. "You heard all that?"

"I couldn't help but hear." Kalen lifted her chin with a single finger. "If he's close by, he's already seen us together. I didn't want to bring danger to you, Faunalyn. I'm sorry."

Faunalyn rolled her eyes and snorted. "Quit that nonsense now, buddy. I already said we're in this together." She looked past him, then rose up and surprised him with a kiss on the lips. In public. "Don't make me be any more obvious. These parents might not like their little ones seeing such displays of affection. And if Hamstead is watching, let him simmer in that a bit. Now, I need to pick up my mail, then we can grab some ice cream from I Scream and stop by Delaney's to get Vivian a chocolate treat, since she's not with us to enjoy the day."

The universe let itself be known to him in her eyes, a sign that they were a match. The magic of it didn't matter. Ultimately, it was her fearless heart and her unwavering resolve to stand by his side that won him.

Chapter 14

Behind the smile and childlike curiosity, Kalen's unease never settled from the moment they left Hats in the Belfry. The sheer joy he expressed when he took his first lick of rum-laced ice cream set her heart fluttering in her chest, but it couldn't wash away the faint shadows in his eyes. He had shed his sunglasses shortly after Hank called, and hadn't bothered with them since. She wasn't sure if it was because the clouds started to roll in or if he just didn't care about a disguise. Either way, she preferred looking into his diamond-laced blue eyes. This sign of newly acquired confidence fed her a bit of joy.

After a quick stop at Magical Mayhem to pick up the mail, check her equipment, and slip the circlet into her safe behind the wall panels between some storage shelves, Fawn felt a little more at ease. Especially if they were, in fact, being followed.

Fawn was surprised when they went to Delaney's Delectables and found that Delaney wasn't working. She'd secretly hoped to get the inside scoop on Hugh's progress regarding a prospective cure for Vivian. She recognized one of the two teenagers as a friend of Wendy's and waved as she approached the glass display case with numerous different Delaney creations. The sweet, rich scent of the shop alone made her jaw ache.

"Hi, Fawn. Nice to see you again. Wendy told me you were taking a small break from your shop. A well-deserved one." Nicole, if Fawn remembered the girl's name correctly, lifted her brows as her gaze shifted to Kalen. "*Very* well deserved."

"Hoping to get back to work soon," Fawn said. As much as she wanted the time to research the Celestial fae, she longed to get her shop open and see the smiles of the children who came in for her smoothies. "Where's Delaney?"

"Oh, she had something to do with the baby. She'll be back soon. Want me to tell her you stopped by?"

"Nah. I'll touch base with her later. I wanted to get some delicacies." She nodded toward Kalen. "We have a Delaney's Delectables virgin here."

Nicole's eyes widened. "Oh, that's unacceptable! What will it be?"

Fawn rattled off an order of three different kinds of fudge, caramel-filled and cherry-filled chocolates, half a dozen of the daily brownie special, and sugared fruit bites. When she caught Kalen scrutinizing two gift bags of brittle, she added them to her purchase.

"I think that'll do," Fawn said. To Kalen, she asked, "Is there anything else that catches your eye?"

He cast her a shaded glance, one brow lifting slowly. Yeah, maybe she should have rephrased that question.

"I think you're outdoing yourself. I hope you intend to help me with all of this," he said, his voice a notch lower and huskier than usual. "Had I suspected you'd buy half the store, I would have asked to stop at the bank first."

Fawn laughed, more to hide her sudden warmth. Damn the man. "Wouldn't happen."

"Fawn is stubborn. Once she has her mind made up, nothing and no one can change it," Nicole said.

"I've noticed. Quite an endearing characteristic."

And if Nicole wasn't heart-eyes for Kalen to start, the moment he smiled, Fawn swore she witnessed the poor girl's lungs deflate before she composed herself. She didn't blame her. Kalen's smile was sheer magic.

Fawn paid for her purchases, said her farewells, and left with Kalen close by her side.

"You're still tense," she said quietly as they headed to her car.

"I still feel we're being watched. I can't pinpoint exactly where it's coming from, and that bothers me." Kalen sighed, taking the bag of treats from Fawn. He hung it on his wrist, along with their bag of hats. "I need to get back to my sister, but I won't leave you alone."

His protective behavior—as evidenced in little things, from the angle of his body to the gentle touches on her arms or back—filled her with dreamy ideas. At the same time, she slowly came to realize that Kalen was the first man to ever make her want something more than her independence and the freedom to do as she chose. She wanted someone to share her successes and failures with. Someone who she could laugh with over dinners or watch sunrises with for years to come.

First, they had to find Hamstead, put an end to the mad scientist's threat, and get Vivian well.

"Why don't you check in on her and then come back to my place? By then, I should have heard something from Hugh."

As much as she wanted to suggest tagging along, she wouldn't do something to compromise the siblings' hideaway. The way Kalen's lips tightened and a small crease formed over his brow told her he battled with his decisions. Geez, what she would give to show him a hard decision was between a protein-based chocolate smoothie and a delicious frozen dragon fruit granola bowl.

"You missed my saying I wasn't leaving you alone."

"No, I heard that quite clearly, actually. But the fact remains that your sister needs you and I'm perfectly capable of handling myself. I've got people here watching out for me. For us." She took his free hand between her own and kissed his fingertips. She smiled up at him when his gaze shot to her. "I'll go hang at Howler's or something. I'll stay busy. Do what you need to do."

At last, he nodded. A small, reluctant tip of his head.

Fawn almost regretted her suggestion as she

watched Kalen's joy slip from his eyes and his aura, leaving a troubled man in its stead. The drive to her house was fraught with tension. She found herself looking in her rearview mirror more than the road in front of her. Only when Kalen rested his hand over hers did she relax a little. Still, her shoulders remained stiff and her senses wary.

"Come with me," he said quietly.

Fawn blinked. She shook her head. "No. That's not a good idea."

"None of this is a good idea, Faunalyn."

A sweet chill unfurled along her skin. The man never did listen to her when she told him to call her Fawn, and every time he spoke her full name, it was like listening to forbidden temptation in the way of the spoken language.

"But not because this isn't supposed to be." He eased her hand over so he could trace the lines along her palm. His airy touch unleashed faint waves of tingles up her arm. "Together, right?"

The smile that crossed her lips was nothing shy of genuine. "Together."

"Are you crazy?" Jackson tore his hands through his ruffled hair. Again. "You *are* crazy. Completely nuts. You could blow this entire plan out of the water."

Kalen rolled his eyes to the ceiling of the cabin and groaned inwardly. Any moment now, he expected

Jackson to fall through the wooden floor he was leaving tread marks on. The man's incessant pacing made Kalen dizzy.

"What if you were followed? What if…what if…I don't know what to say."

"So it seems," Kalen groused.

"Hey, I've done nothing but help you out. I've risked my neck for you and Vivian, and you go and steal my car to return to Nocturne Falls, knowing the danger there." Jackson growled. Or at least, Kalen believed that's what the squeak was supposed to be. Between the man's half-hiss, half-squeal scolding, Kalen wasn't certain. Jackson swung a hand toward the bag from Delaney's Delectables on the table, along with the silly hats. "And you went into town? In? To? *Town*? Kalen, what were you thinking?"

Kalen scowled. He was about to answer when Jackson wagged a finger in his face.

"I'll tell you what you were thinking. You weren't!"

Kalen arched his brows and folded his arms over his chest. "Are you through?"

"No!" Jackson made two laps between the kitchen table and Kalen, then fell into one of the chairs. "Damn it, Kalen! You can't be that careless. Not now. Not when we're so close to figuring out a cure for your sister."

"Do you think I'm really so careless as to jeopardize the welfare of my own sister?" Kalen asked.

Jackson leaned to the side, exaggerating his motion to look past Kalen toward the bedroom where Faunalyn had gone to see Vivian.

"Must I answer that for you?" He shook his head once and pinched the bird's nest hat, lifting it from the table. "Really?" He dropped it on the table and pulled the treat bag closer. Jackson rummaged through the boxes of chocolates and candies until he pulled out one of the bags of brittle. "Oh, this is my favorite."

"Help yourself," Kalen muttered as Jackson opened the bag and took out a piece of the chocolate and peanut treat. He held up a hand when Jackson offered the bag out to him. "I find my appetite lacking at the moment."

"'Cause you know I'm right about you screwing up," Jackson said through a mouthful of brittle. "Not that I blame you."

"I don't understand you at times. Do you or don't you condone my actions? And do you plan on rambling on all evening about my careless decisions?"

"I didn't say I condoned your decision to return to town. What I said was that I didn't blame you for doing so, if the reason for your return is giving Vivian another dose of magical sedative as we speak." Jackson dug out another piece of candy. "I know many a man who's made a pass at her. She's pretty untouchable. Just a warning."

Kalen couldn't mask the subtle half-grin that crept over his lips. Jackson stopped chewing the brittle, his eyes widening.

"No way." He shook his half-eaten candy at Kalen. "No, you didn't."

"Did what?" He was honestly baffled. The spark in Jackson's eyes, though, triggered a very vivid idea. Oh, did *that*. "No."

It was none of Jackson's business what happened between him and Faunalyn. Despite the smirk that grew on the man's mouth, he had the decency to lift a hand in surrender and shrug.

"Not my concern. Well, yeah. It kinda is if you plan on stealing my car more often. But just know that she's pretty well protected by the bigwigs in town. She has a successful business and is very well connected." He bit off another piece of brittle. "So, don't jump into anything you don't plan on finishing. If I were in your predicament, I wouldn't jump into anything at all right now."

Kalen pressed his lips together. Jackson had a point. He knew he should never have let his curiosity about Faunalyn keep him going back to her. He shouldn't have dragged her into this mess.

He never knew how weak a man could become when his heart was involved. If there was one poignant lesson he learned with Faunalyn, it was this.

Standing in the kitchen, watching Jackson devour the bag of brittle, he couldn't bring himself to regret anything he'd done. Not when it came to Faunalyn.

He released a low breath, twisted on his heel, and left Jackson to finish the brittle with smoke coming out of his ears. Literally. Kalen knew the man was part witch, but he'd never before witnessed his magic. He feared if he didn't walk away, he'd start laughing.

Instead, he stopped by Vivian's ajar bedroom door. Through the crack, he saw Vivian sat cross-legged on the bed. Faunalyn mirrored the position in front of his sister, the box of Delaney's brownies between them. It was the first time in weeks he'd witnessed his sister's genuine smile, one that lit her eyes and brightened her beautiful face. A faint glow illuminated her skin, so faint he doubted anyone other than a vampire would notice. The sun was only starting to descend into dusk, but the outline of the round moon hung high in the sky, waiting its turn to shine.

His spirit soared as he listened to Faunalyn talk about Nocturne Falls, painting the town so vividly with her words and descriptions. Vivian's joy intensified, her excitement almost childlike. She popped small pieces of brownie into her mouth, licking the crumbs from her fingertips. Her eyes widened when Faunalyn described the town's center with the gargoyle fountain and manicured lawns.

"A *real* gargoyle?" Vivian gasped.

Faunalyn laughed. "Most of the time, yes. They have a statue to substitute for the real deal on occasion. They're magnificent creatures. I can't wait to bring you around at night. The town is lit up like a fairytale. It's like walking into a different world. There are street shows and costumes, and just a magical feel to everything."

"Has Kalen seen it? Oh, how he deserves such wonders."

Faunalyn rested a hand on Vivian's knee. "You both deserve it, and you'll both have it. Soon. With only

Hamstead to worry about now, and a potential cure for whatever that monster injected into you near completion, you'll be able to walk the streets freely, without having to fear for your life. All of the things that have been kept from you, you'll have. I promise."

Kalen seldom experienced the burn of tears, but the emotion behind Faunalyn's promise, and the sight of his sister's chin quivering before she threw her arms around his woman's neck, delivered a punch he wasn't prepared for.

"Thank you, Fawn."

Kalen bit down on his lower lip and lowered his head. He listened to his sister's soft sniffles until Faunalyn's sweet, magical voice began to hum a soothing tune. When he looked into the room again, breath hitched at the alluring song, he stared at the woman who gave him hope, dared him to dream, and laid claim to his heart. Her eyes were closed as she rocked with Vivian, humming a calming melody.

He rested his head on the doorjamb, his body relaxing as the song seemed to ease beneath his skin and into his muscles. Unlike the song that drew out the desire in him, this one called up comfort. The tune itself was a sanctuary of promise and hope.

Caught up in the melody, he hadn't realized Faunalyn's eyes had opened. She watched him, her hand smoothing over Vivian's pale hair. Her gaze was as magical as her voice, luring him closer.

He moved as if drawn by the magic of her song, stepping up to the side of the bed before he could stop himself. Vivian lifted her head as he reached for Faunalyn's cheek, caressing her skin with the back of his hand.

"Faunalyn," he murmured.

Vivian took hold of his other hand, kissing his knuckles. She straightened off Faunalyn as his darling woman ended her song. He couldn't resist leaning down and pressing a soft kiss to Faunalyn's mouth.

"I think I've taken her from you long enough, brother."

Kalen grinned against Faunalyn's mouth before he leaned back and lowered himself to the bed.

Vivian's cheeks took on a snowy rose color, her lower lip caught between her teeth. He hadn't thought about how his actions might have made his sister uncomfortable.

"My apologies, Vivi. I shouldn't have done that," Kalen said, giving his sister's hand a squeeze. "She wanted to spend time with you, and you deserve the gift of her presence. I shouldn't have interrupted."

"Are you feeling better?" Faunalyn asked Vivian.

"Much. Your touch is pure magic. Thank you." A smile spread over his sister's lips and her gaze moved between Kalen and Faunalyn. He couldn't help the burst of possession that claimed him when Faunalyn leaned into his chest. "Oh, Kalen. I never imagined I'd see the day when you looked so genuinely at ease. Fawn, you've given my brother life, and I could never repay you for that gift. It's all I've ever wanted for him. He's never put himself first ever since we were taken by the Lab Coats. His life was me, taking care of me, protecting me. And now, to see him so happy?" She sighed. "Thank you for that."

"I don't think that was all my doing," Faunalyn said. "You know, you're very lucky to have a brother like him. His dedication to you is commendable."

"It's stolen his life."

"*Hamstead* stole my life. Your life," Kalen corrected. He was about to continue when Faunalyn's phone buzzed from her purse on the floor. He reached down and retrieved it, taking note of the number. "Here."

Faunalyn answered. This time, Kalen decided to keep his ears out of the conversation. Instead, he traced Vivian's brow and smiled.

"It's a relief to see you like this, Vivi."

"Me? Have you seen yourself? You're glowing."

Kalen chuckled. "I think that's part of what we are. The Celestial part of us."

Vivian's smile turned into something sly. "So, mother was right. Did you see the universe?" Kalen couldn't believe the warmth that brushed his cheeks. Vivian nudged his arm. "You did."

"Yes."

"Oh, this makes me even more happy for you."

Faunalyn ended the call, her smile stunning. "Well, I think you're going to be getting your life back." Those lavender-gold eyes turned up to Kalen. "Tonight."

Chapter 15

They waited for night to fall before leaving the cabin and heading into Nocturne Falls. Kalen refused to let her drive her car alone, taking the driver's seat before she made it out the door. Fawn crossed her arms over her chest and raised a brow.

"What?" he asked.

"You know what."

Kalen flashed her a smile and closed the door. Fawn groaned, rolling her eyes to the sky.

"Yeah. Good luck with that," Jackson said, tossing his keys in the air. "Guess the royal thing is going to his head, huh?"

"I heard that," Kalen said loudly.

Jackson gave him an exaggerated double thumbs up. "Good, buddy."

Fawn snickered. "You two bicker like brothers, you know that?" She started to round the front of the car, giving Kalen a hard glower through the windshield. "If we don't make it to Hugh's by nine, come looking for us around a tree."

Kalen's lips pulled back in a wry smile. She flashed him a cheeky grin before pulling open the passenger side door. Over the roof, she waved to Vivian as the woman settled into Jackson's car, then slipped into the passenger seat.

"The only reason I crashed that night was because Vivi attacked me and I couldn't correct the car." Kalen's defensive explanation caught Fawn off guard. She watched him twist the key in the ignition as she pulled the door closed. He looked awfully comfortable behind the wheel. He lanced her with a warm glance. "If there is anyone you're safe with when it comes to driving, and just about anything else, it's me."

Fawn gasped when he popped the car into drive and slammed his foot down on the accelerator, causing the car to jump forward.

"Yeah, sure," she squeaked.

The tires spun out on the dirt path. She could almost hear Jackson swearing up a storm as dirt and pebbles pelted the front of his car.

Kalen chuckled. "He's so easy to needle." Another side-glance at her and his chuckle turned into a laugh. "Don't tell me you are, too."

"You know, he thinks you hate him," Fawn said, relaxing as Kalen steadied out the car and reached a cruising speed. Quite a bit faster than she would have preferred, though. "Or at least have a distinguished distaste for him."

"I have a distaste for most people." He shook his head. "No, more like distrust. I don't trust people, but I trust him. I'm comfortable with him. I don't have to pretend to be or feel something to protect myself and my sister with him. Nor with you."

Fawn laid her hand over his on the shifter. "Most people would take scowls and a cool attitude in a negative way. Perhaps you should try being, um, less aggressive and more friendly."

Kalen's jaw moved, darkening the hollows of cheeks already dressed in shadows as his skin took on a luminescent glow beneath the moonlight. It wasn't as bright as it had been the night before, but the essence of his fae roots was undeniable.

"Should I buy him roses and chocolate?" Kalen asked.

Fawn burst out laughing. The corner of his mouth twitched before his lips curled upward.

"*That* might be taken the wrong way. No, Kalen. I'd suggest you laugh with him. Mess around with him without picking on him. Don't get so overly defensive when he asks a question. He's asking because he genuinely wants to know."

"So I should have told him what occurred between us last night?" Fawn choked. Her face went from cool to boiling in a half-second. "He asked. Actually, he implied in question." He flipped his hand around and wove his fingers between hers as she struggled to fix the burning thermostat in her body. "I would never tell anyone what happens between us."

"Good. That's reassuring."

Kalen lifted her hand and kissed her knuckles. Spirits, this man knew just what to do to make her melt.

"Tell me, Faunalyn. When this is through, when Hamstead is gone and Vivian is cured, how would you feel about me sticking around?"

She swallowed hard. This was a talk she hadn't thought about having so soon, but now that he brought it up, it was as good a time as any. "You wouldn't want to try and learn more about your mother's side of the family? The royal fae?"

Kalen shrugged. "If the information comes to me, then I'll be fine with it. I have no intention of searching for a family that abandoned my mother and left us in cells at the hands of a monster. I'm content being who I am. I know I'm different, and I understand with my differences may come curiosity and questions and even shunning. I'm okay with that."

She was floored. What descendant of royalty didn't want to know more about their family line? Who wouldn't want to learn more about the very fabric of what created them?

"You seem taken aback," Kalen said quietly. "Was there a different response you were expecting?"

"I, um, I'm not sure. Definitely not that one."

"Crowns and prestige and all that glamor doesn't appeal to me. What I want, what I've dreamed of, is freedom. That is all. The ability to live and not look over my shoulder. The chance to sit at a restaurant and sip wine and enjoy a gourmet meal. The freedom to walk out of my house and feel the sun on my face or stare at the moon, now that I've seen what it looks like when it's full. The opportunity to have friends." He looked at her. "Have a woman I could start a family with. I have dreams, Faunalyn. Simple dreams that I have come to realize most people take for granted. Anything else is a gift, and I'd gladly accept it. With that said, would you kindly answer my question? Would you like me to stay in Nocturne Falls?"

"Stay?" Silly question, because she dreaded the thought of him leaving. She dared not think about the time when he would say goodbye and their special moments together would be nothing more than memories. "What do you think?"

"If the shimmer in your eyes is any indication, I'd say yes."

"I'm not going to cry, so don't get your hopes up." The sting in her eyes threatened to turn her into a liar. "And you should be watching the road, not my eyes."

"I can't help myself. I see all of my hopes and dreams in the universe of your eyes."

"So romantic." Any other guy, she'd have rolled her eyes a million times by now, but Kalen's compliments were as raw and from the heart as they came. The man hadn't been corrupted by the real world enough to throw meaningless words at her. "Yes. I'd love for you to stay. You and Vivian. The residents of Nocturne Falls would help you acclimate to life in town. One of my two employees will be heading off to college in another month or so. I'll need some extra hands at the shop. Wendy would love to teach you both how things go. I'm sure if that doesn't work out, we can get you a job elsewhere."

"Are you certain us working together would be a good idea?" Kalen's eyes stayed on the road, but he brushed his lips over her knuckles again. His brow rose. "We've already had two close encounters in the back of the shop."

Fawn groaned, dropping her head back against the seat. "You're killing me, Kalen."

"I'll be more considerate for the next few hours."

"Good. When this is over, you can be as inconsiderate as you want. For now, we need to make sure we get to Hugh's without Hamstead popping up."

The trip to Hugh Ellingham's house was uneventful, except for Kalen's occasional teasing remarks. Fawn made a mental note to ask him at a later date about what kind of movies he occupied his time with over the last few decades. She wasn't sure whether to laugh or cringe at a few of the comments coming from his mouth.

"Before we get to Hugh's, there are a few things I should mention. About vampires," Fawn said, dragging the conversation away from Kalen's recollection of an Alfred Hitchcock movie he'd seen, triggered by turning onto Hitchcock Lane. "Hugh is one of three grandsons of Eleanora Ellingham. She pretty much owns Nocturne Falls. The boys run different aspects of town, from business to entertainment, and such. Hugh has a butler of sorts. Stanhill. He's what vampires call a 'rook.' He's not completely turned, but he's been made virtually immortal. I don't know all the logistics behind turnings, but that might be something we can ask tonight. Stanhill will be helping us. Delaney is Hugh's wife and very friendly, so try to be friendly back. She's not Jackson."

"I'm quite aware of what is expected of me."

"Good. Because we're here."

Fawn pointed to Hugh's mansion. She had always been astounded by the homes in this area, the shameless wealth presented in perfectly manicured lawns and fine-tuned details around each house. Hugh Ellingham was pretty humble for his extravagant wealth. Delaney had made him even more so.

Jackson pulled into the driveway behind them. Fawn and Kalen waited for Jackson and Vivian to join them before climbing the stairs to the wrap-around porch.

The door opened before Fawn had a chance to knock. Stanhill greeted them with a smile.

"Fawn, such a pleasure to see you." The handsome older man's sharp gaze cruised over Kalen, Vivian, then Jackson before returning to her. "Come in. Hugh is thrilled to finally meet your friends. It's been all he's talked about over the last few days."

Fawn accepted Stanhill's invitation and led everyone into the spacious entry foyer. "I can't begin to thank him enough for offering to help out. I had no idea he held an interest in chemistry and biology."

Stanhill snickered. "He's full of surprises. Can I offer you something to drink? I believe Delaney just finished a fresh batch of cookies."

"Of course I did," Delaney said, rounding a corner with a tray in hand. Her eyes lit up and a smile spread over her mouth. Her chestnut hair was tied up in a messy knot and she had flour smudges on her cheeks. "I couldn't let you come here without treats to offer. Here. They're my latest creation. Double chocolate cayenne cookies. There's a little bite to them. I hope that's okay."

"Anything you make is spectacular." Fawn helped herself to a cookie. "I think I've forgotten my manners. Delaney, Stanhill, let me introduce Kalen and Vivian Hawkins, and Jackson Emery."

"So nice to meet you. Hugh's been talking incessantly about 'the duo' since Hank explained your dilemma. He's simply dumbfounded that you can walk during the day without some kind of magical help," Delaney said, stretching out the tray to Kalen and Vivian.

Fawn took a bite of her cookie, warm and gooey with a hint of spice, and watched Kalen and Vivian debate over the treats. Jackson reached through the two, picked off one cookie, and ate it in a couple of quick bites. Kalen murmured something in his native language to Vivian, who smiled and picked the largest cookie from the tray.

"Thank you, Delaney," she said quietly, bringing the cookie to her nose. She sniffed the treat, then took a tentative bite. The moment her eyes widened in delight, Delaney giggled. "Oh my. It's delicious."

"It's a unique flavor and hard to come by. Stanhill?" Delaney held the tray out for the rook, who politely declined. "He's been taste testing these most of the afternoon. I wanted to get them right before you showed up. Well, Hugh's in the basement. His lab is down there. What do you say?" Delaney's smile swung to Vivian. "Ready to get better?"

Chapter 16

Kalen cautiously followed Faunalyn into the basement lab, which looked nothing like the labs he was used to. Far from cold and sterile, whites and metals, this lab had a comforting warmth to it with its dark wood accents and leather furniture. He had taken the opportunity to observe the woman, Delaney, while testing out her cookies, and noticed similarities to himself in her. The paler skin and sharp eyes, of course. She didn't move at lightning speed, but her movements were fluid as she practically floated down the stairs. He tried to ignore the curiosity he noted in her gaze as she looked him over, then turned her acute attention on Vivian.

As they approached the tall man with dark hair and piercing blue eyes standing by a table with test tubes and hot plates, he endured the same curious scrutiny. Only the man he assumed was Hugh Ellingham was less subtle in his observation than his wife.

Kalen stepped around the rays of moonlight coming through a basement window. His skin was luminescent enough without any help from the moon's magic. He didn't have the answers for the questions churning in Hugh's expression.

Hugh held out his hand. "Good evening. I'm Hugh Ellingham. I see you've met Delaney."

Kalen nodded, shaking the vampire's hand. His skin was cool, his grip strong. His English accent wasn't thick, but it was evident.

"Thank you for offering to help my sister," Kalen said. Until he witnessed Vivian's recovery, he would hold a sliver of doubt. He didn't understand how these people willingly opened their doors to help two strangers accused of killing an innocent man. The people of Nocturne Falls took Fawn at her word, which ultimately was his word. "Her welfare means the world to me."

"So I've heard. Let's hope this works. I've read over all the notes and test results Jackson provided from his uncle and himself. Using those, with the latest findings compliments of Fawn's magic, I think I've developed something that might stop the progression of the virus and start reversing the effects. Judging by the results I've obtained through my experiments, if all goes well, Vivian should be symptom free within three to five days." Hugh grinned. "Fawn, would you be willing to offer another touch of your elven magic to help the process along once I've administered this injection?"

"No need to ask." Fawn tipped her chin upward. Kalen filled with pride. "Anything to help her get well."

"Very good. Stanhill, would you finish fixing up one of the spare rooms?" As the rook nodded and took his leave of the group, Hugh turned to Vivian. "I think it would be best if you stay here until the process is complete. I'll need to give you one injection a day. If you are in agreement, I would like to follow the injections with blood work."

Vivian stepped around Kalen. "That would be fine. I'm just grateful this is going to come to an end. One I hadn't expected."

Hugh rested his hands on Vivian's shoulders. Kalen stiffened until Fawn entwined her hand in his, providing a dose of calm through his fingers. He glanced down at her and earned a reassuring grin.

"We will do everything we can to make sure you are free of this thing that was put inside you. The man responsible will be brought to justice." Hugh lifted his gaze to Kalen. "I've gone one step further, my friend. My brother has contacted an agency close to the laboratory to notify them of the illegal experiments being performed. The lab should be shut down in no time. There will be no more experiments on paranormals within those walls."

Kalen's brows furrowed and he tensed against the tightness growing in his throat. The kindness extended to him and Vivian was beyond his comprehension. "Thank you."

"When this is over, I hope you choose to stay in Nocturne Falls. You'll have a home here. You'll have friends. People you can trust. I hope you come to believe that."

Kalen's heart thudded when he turned back to Faunalyn. Yes. He knew he had everything he could ever want, ever dream of, as long as this woman was by his side. "Thank you, Hugh. I've become aware of the gift that is Nocturne Falls and the people who reside here."

Faunalyn leaned into his arm and nuzzled her cheek against his sleeve.

"Well, then. Are we ready?" Hugh asked, clapping his hands together. Kalen was surprised to see his sister smile, her eyes filled with joy. There wasn't a speck of fear or doubt in her face, in her composure. Only hope.

Vivian slipped out of her cloak, draped it over Jackson's outstretched arm, and followed Hugh to an upholstered chair at the end of his worktable. Kalen watched in silent apprehension as Hugh drew a light yellow liquid into an antique-looking syringe.

"This might sting, but it shouldn't last," Hugh said, flicking the bubbles to the top of the syringe and expelling the last of the air. He wiped Vivian's arm with alcohol—the scent brought a rush of dreadful memories to mind, forcing Kalen to stop breathing until the scent dissipated—and eased the needle into her arm. Vivian didn't so much as flinch, watching as Hugh injected the liquid into her body. Kalen refrained from stopping him, a natural instinct from the years of testing. More warmth fluttered up through his hand and arm, constant and serene. Faunalyn knew exactly what he needed, and what to do to keep him calm.

"All done." Hugh straightened and placed the syringe on the table. "Delaney will show you to your room. I suggest that Fawn might want to give you some of her sedative magic. I would like to take a blood sample in a few hours to see if the antidote is working."

Vivian wiggled her fingers, her eyes wide with wonder. "Yes, yes. I would like to know, too."

Faunalyn gave Kalen's hand a gentle squeeze, then went to help Vivian out of the chair. Delaney, who had given up her tray of cookies to Stanhill to take upstairs, took Vivian's hand.

"You'll have a beautiful view from your room," Delaney said as she led Vivian toward the stairs.

Kalen was tempted to follow, simply to make sure his sister was well cared for, although he knew she would be in the best hands between Faunalyn and Delaney. Instead, he focused on Hugh as the vampire played with a few of the test tubes.

"I'm awfully curious about you, Kalen. I'm not going to lie. That you can walk in daylight without help from a talisman or amulet is quite amazing," Hugh said. He placed the test tube he was swirling back into a holder and brushed his hands on his pants. His brows lifted as his gaze landed on Jackson. "If I may, I'd like to speak with Kalen for a few minutes in private."

Jackson nodded, shifting uneasily. "Oh, yeah. Sure. I'll, uh, I'll be upstairs." He shuffled toward the stairs, shoulders slouched as if the air in his lungs abandoned him.

"If you don't mind, Hugh, I would prefer Jackson to remain here. If there is anything you wish to discuss, I assure you, it can be discussed with him present," Kalen said.

Jackson glanced over his shoulder, and the look that crossed his face brought an easy smile to Kalen's mouth. He nodded once at Jackson, humored by the young man's shock.

"Very well. I suppose he is good at keeping secrets." Hugh motioned to a few chairs set up in an arrangement across the room. "Shall we?"

Kalen settled into a chair as Hugh poured two glasses of red wine. Jackson sat rigid and tense until Kalen arched a brow at him.

"Can I offer you a drink, Jackson?"

"Um, water?"

Hugh chuckled. "I have liquor."

"Whatever you've got, then."

Hugh nodded and poured a shot of something amber into a glass, then joined them. He handed out the drinks before taking a seat. "The wine is a special blend. I hope you enjoy it."

Kalen lifted the glass and took a small sniff, followed by a cautious taste. His gaze narrowed on Hugh. "Is this what I think it is?"

Hugh nodded. "For our kind."

The coppery essence of blood laced in the depth of fruit flavors was undeniable. It made his jaw ache as he drank, satiating the thirst he was becoming familiar with. Though, if he were to admit, nothing compared to the taste of Faunalyn. This would be a temporary fix, but he wanted so badly to have her offer him another drink.

"I've spent a long time trying to find a way for vampires to walk in the sunlight. I've never been successful," Hugh said, swirling the wine in his glass. "I've never met a vampire-fae either. Goes to show that even living through a few centuries, there is much I've yet to learn. Would you share with me how you feel when you walk out in the sun?"

"I saw you in town. You walk in the sun," Kalen pointed out. "I'm sure my reaction is no different from yours."

"Are you sensitive to it?"

"It can irritate me, especially my eyes, but it doesn't do much else."

"Do you know much about your fae roots?"

Kalen shook his head. "No. I only found out my specific race yesterday."

"There's little documented history about the Celestial fae. I've been doing research and coming up empty," Jackson added. A flash of guilt slipped through his gaze as Kalen looked at him. The man cleared his throat. "My uncle, the man killed by Hamstead and his cronies, sent me the only information he had. He gathered it from Mauryn before she was killed."

"Mauryn?" Kalen asked. A strange, sickening wave stirred in his belly. Jackson pressed his lips together and nodded.

"Mauryn was your mother's name."

His mother, whose true name he never knew.

"Nicholas knew my mother?" Kalen asked. Nicholas never once confided in him that he had known his mother. "Why hadn't he told me?"

Jackson began to play with the cloak draped over his legs. "The less you knew about your mother and her lineage, the safer you and Vivian would be. He was going to tell you everything once you arrived at my house, but...well, he didn't make it."

Kalen tilted his head. "How long have *you* known this information?"

"Uncle Nick had a certified letter scheduled to arrive at my house. In case something happened to him. I received it right before we left for the cabin. That's why I gave the circlet to Faunalyn. I figured it was safest with her, since at the time, there was really no connection between you and her that would have caused Hamstead to tail her. Hamstead doesn't know your family descends from royalty. If he found out?" Jackson let out a sharp breath. "The guy's power hungry enough. Imagine what he'd do to get his hands on you both if he knew the powers you had locked inside you."

"What do you know about Kalen's powers?" Hugh asked.

"Yes," Kalen added. "What do you know about me?"

"Well, um, with a little work, you have the ability to create destinies and manipulate time and space to control the destinies of others. It's a particular power granted to the High Guard of the Celestial fae to keep order in the universe."

Kalen swallowed. He glanced at Hugh. The man's eyes widened before cutting to Kalen.

"I have the letter in safe keeping, Kalen. I didn't want to chance Hamstead getting hold of it, knowing he was snooping around." The corner of Jackson's mouth tugged down. "I didn't keep it from you intentionally. The focus was your sister, then getting out of town before Hamstead arrived. The last few days, I all but forgot the letter."

Kalen remained silent as he worked through the alien emotions swirling inside him. He wasn't certain that Jackson betrayed him, but he withheld important information from him. Information that could have answered many of his questions days ago. With each small piece of the fae puzzle coming together, he realized just how dangerous Hamstead could be to him and Vivian.

If he ever found out the truth.

"How long did Nicholas know my mother?" Kalen asked.

"According to the letter, he knew your mother from the first time she was caught and placed in captivity. When Hamstead introduced your father to her in hopes of creating an anomaly."

"My sister and I."

Jackson nodded, his eyes lowering. "He accepted the offer for the position not fully comprehending what he was a part of. He believed he was going to be part of a team developing a cure for some of the world's deadliest illnesses. You know, cancer, genetic diseases, those types of things. When he realized what was going on—my uncle was never one to do jobs blindly, so he looked deeper into the lab's foundation—he was going to leave. Then he met your mother. He decided to stay solely to protect her.

"He helped her and your father escape, and stayed behind until he resigned his position. Uncle Nick kept in contact with your mother over the years. He feared that Hamstead might have caught on to him and traced him back to your mother, and that's how you and Vivian were captured and your parents were killed. When he was asked to come back to his old position a few years after you and Vivian were taken into captivity, he hesitated, but did it only because he had a duty to you and your sister."

Jackson leaned forward and said earnestly, "Kalen, he swore he would protect you and Vivian the best he could. The letter explains everything in more detail, but that's the gist of it."

The silence that hung over the men was palpable. Jackson continued to fiddle with the edge of Vivi's cloak, his gaze averted. Hugh sipped his wine, his expression unreadable.

Kalen sat back in his seat.

Everyone has secrets, Kalen. Sometimes, it's best to leave the secrets be. But don't think for a moment that there isn't more to the story than what you've been told.

Nicholas had secrets. Secrets he never disclosed to Kalen. Secrets that directly affected him and Vivian. One of the first men Kalen trusted withheld the key to the source of his existence and never told him a thing.

"Everything my uncle did was to protect you and Vivian. I think he knew he wasn't going to survive the escape, but he was content with his decision and didn't regret it," Jackson finally said. "The scheduled arrival of the letter, the emails, his lab notes. He knew in his gut he wasn't going to survive. Hamstead is a snake. He's a monster. Look at what he's done to you and Vivian. He has no problem sleeping at night, Kalen. If he had no restrictions, imagine what evil he'd be capable of."

"Seems we need to find this Hamstead, fast," Hugh said.

"Yes." Kalen nodded once, emotions churning. "The nightmare has gone on long enough, and now he wants to bring it here. Into this town." He stood up and placed his glass on a small table between him and Hugh. Catching the vampire's eyes, he added, "I won't let that happen."

Whether he was faster than the vampire, or if Hugh decided to give him a head start, he'd never know. Within seconds, he was far beyond the bounds of Hugh Ellingham's house, running as fast as he could straight into town.

Hamstead wanted him. He wanted Vivian.

Very well.

Too many people had sacrificed things for them. Too many people were willing to sacrifice more. He wouldn't let that happen. He wanted a life, and he wanted it now.

If obtaining life was through death, then so be it. No one else would be hurt.

Kalen came to the edge of Main Street and slowed down. He had no disguise. No jacket. No sunglasses. Only the clothes on his back and his boots.

Yes, he earned glances. Many glances, with his faintly glowing skin and eyes.

Kalen stepped off the sidewalk and started a slow stride away from the busy storefronts.

"If you want me, Hamstead, I'm right here," he murmured. "Come and get me."

Chapter 17

"Where did he go?" Fawn felt panicked when Jackson told her of Kalen's abrupt departure. She thanked the gods she had given Vivian another dose of magic, because the woman was sleeping right through this mess. "Why didn't you stop him?"

Jackson snorted. He lifted his hands to his sides, palms up, and imitated a scale. "Vampire, witch. Vampire, witch." He wiggled the fingers on the hand sitting lower. "Like I could've stopped him."

Delaney rested a hand on her shoulder. "Hank's got his men out looking for him. Hugh won't let anything happen to him."

Fawn rubbed her hands over her face. Her stomach flipped, threatening to relieve her of the cookies she had enjoyed so much. "I should try to find him."

"That's crazy," Jackson said.

"Well, *he's* not acting too sane, if you ask me." Fawn groaned.

"Hugh doesn't want you leaving. Not until they've found Kalen."

Like she'd stay put. Fawn sighed and nodded in resignation. "Okay. Fine. But I need my purse. I want to try to call him."

"He doesn't have a phone," Jackson said, suspicion filling his tone.

"That changed earlier today."

Goddess, forgive me for lying. Thankfully, the bite of guilt for the small lie was overpowered by the urgency to find Kalen. She had a sinking feeling he was on a mission that could end up with him dead.

"I'll go with you."

Fawn pinned Jackson with a hard glower. "I don't need a babysitter."

"Just to make sure." Jackson smiled and held out his arm. "Let's go."

To Fawn's relief, Delaney remained in the bedroom with Vivian. She tried to keep as relaxed as possible, but the closer they came to the foyer where she had left her purse on a table, the more she tensed. Jackson watched her with the attention of a hawk.

"I know you're not one to sit back and wait for things to resolve themselves. Please, don't try to run. If anything happened to you, Kalen would be horrified."

"What makes you think I'd run?" Fawn asked. She gave Jackson's intuition major kudos. And extra points for the below-the-belt tactic of adding Kalen to his plea.

"Unless I trip down the stairs, nothing will happen to me while I fetch my purse."

As they reached the last few steps, Fawn pinpointed her purse, calculated the distance between it and the door, and counted Stanhill's absence a blessing.

Don't hate me. Please don't hate me.

Fawn called up the power of the Earth. Heat and energy coursed through her veins, shifting and flowing up her legs and down her arms.

She released the magic into Jackson, whispering, "I'm sorry."

The man's eyes went wide, his mouth dropping open. His knees buckled. Fawn caught him under his arms and lowered Jackson to the floor as the magic soothed him into sleep.

Heart pounding, Fawn snatched up her purse and bolted from the house. She was in her car and peeling down the road by the time Stanhill ran into the front yard, waving for her to stop.

"What were you thinking, Fawn?" Hank Merrow snapped over the phone.

Fawn scanned the streets of Nocturne Falls, looking for any sign of Kalen. Or, more accurately, any sign of Hamstead. Two laps around the back roads of the residential area came up with nothing. She stopped at her house, found it dark and quiet. She then made her way through the streets of downtown. Nothing.

"Well, you haven't had much luck finding him, either," Fawn groused, turning down Black Cat Boulevard.

"We're trained for these types of situations. You're not. Leave this to us. I don't want to have to worry about saving you, too, if it can be avoided."

The sheriff's authoritative tone merely knocked up her resolve. She had no idea what Kalen had planned, what he was thinking, but something in her gut warned her the outcome of his actions was not going to be good.

"Faunalyn Ayre, you listen to me good. You turn that car around and go back to Hugh's house. You stay there until we've got this figured out, understood?" Hank commanded.

"Yeah, yeah. Sure." *Wishful thinking, Hank.* "In a moment."

"Fawn."

Fawn groaned. "Fine."

"I'll have someone stop by Hugh's house in fifteen minutes. You'd better be there. Otherwise, I'll detain you the minute I find you, if that's what it takes to keep you out of this. You hear?"

Lovely.

"Loud and clear, Sheriff."

"Don't you start that with me. Fifteen minutes."

Hank disconnected the call. Fawn tossed her phone onto the passenger seat as she rounded the corner onto Main Street again. The hour was getting late, but the sidewalks remained crowded with tourists looking for some late-night fun.

If they only knew what was happening right in front of them.

She passed her shop, the hairs along the back of her neck rising. Was the circlet really safe there? Should she stop and get it?

"No."

After another sweep through the tourist district, Fawn spun the car around and started back to Hugh's. Halfway there, she made a last-minute decision to stop at her house one more time. She could only hope Kalen might go there.

As she pulled down the dirt path, she noticed a single light on toward the back of her house. Her heartbeat jumped into overdrive. She cut the engine and nearly sprinted from the car. She threw open the front door.

"Kalen?" Fawn bee-lined to her bedroom, following the soft glow of light.

Her hopes plummeted when she saw the room was empty. If Kalen had stopped here, she had missed him. She glanced toward her desk. Unease settled on her shoulders when she realized Willa's book was missing. She tried to brush the chill away.

Until she heard a click.

Fawn spun around.

"It was only a matter of time before the opportunity presented itself." Hamstead's smile dripped malice and his eyes glowed with pure evil. Fawn stepped back as he advanced on her, the steel barrel of a gun pointed at her head. His other arm held Willa's book clutched to his chest like a child.

Her throat tightened as fear swelled.

"Where's Kalen?" Fawn demanded, but the fierce tone she intended fell short with a tremor.

"We'll find him together."

Ugh, she wanted to slap that smile from his mouth. "What makes you think I can help you? I've been looking for him and unable to find him."

"Oh, come on, Fawn. You're smarter than that."

"You're going to go cliché, aren't you? Use me to lure him. What makes you think that'll work?"

His brows rose in a way that left her chilled to the marrow. "Don't think I haven't been watching you two. You see, I've had many years to watch him. To learn him. What makes him tick. What makes him retreat. I have the means to make him yield to me." His smile melted from malicious to something altogether fearsome. Fawn swallowed the lump choking her throat. "And he *will* yield to me."

"Guess you don't know him as well as you thought. He doesn't yield to anyone."

Hamstead's chuckle raked along her spine. Goddess almighty. This guy was creepy.

"There is a pair of gloves on the bed. Put them on."

"This is Georgia in the middle of the summer—"

The bullet struck the floor a few inches from her feet. She shrieked, jumping back, her skin covered in goose bumps.

"Put the gloves on."

Angry and terrified, Fawn did as she was told, tugging on the thick leather gloves, casting Hamstead glowering glances as she did so.

"Don't think for a moment I'll spare your life. All in the name of science."

"Sick, sick screwball," she muttered. She held up her gloved hands. "Gloved."

"Come here."

Fawn scowled, but did as she was told. Hamstead put the book on the desk and pulled a piece of dark plastic from his pocket with one hand. Her brows furrowed.

"Stop right there. Keep your hands out. Don't you dare move or I'll shoot you."

Fawn fisted her fingers inside the gloves. The guy kept the gun trained on her, right between her eyes. She didn't doubt for a second he would keep his word. Grinding her teeth together, she let him place the plastic bags over her gloved hands. He dug in his back pocket and pulled out a set of handcuffs, snapping them with expert efficiency around her gloved-and-bagged wrists.

"Planning to cast a mold?" Fawn asked. She couldn't help herself. She hated overbearing jerks, and Hamstead fell at the top of the category.

"Watch the lip, lady. I'd hate to split it this early in the game." Hamstead gave the cuffs a hard tug, jerking her forward. Her cheek bumped into his arm. The very contact made her cringe. "I'm aware of your dampening powers, but you can't work your magic through artificial materials, now can you?"

Fawn pressed her lips tight. Oh, how she hated this monster.

"I should thank you for giving me a very important piece of information regarding Kalen and his sister. I knew they were Celestial fae, but I hadn't realized they were royal. You see, Nicholas was a very smart man. A genius. Unfortunately his heart often got the best of him. He was careless when he sent some information to his nephew. My men were able to hack into Jackson's computer and obtain some of the information Nicholas withheld from me, including the significance of Kalen's bloodline. He also was careless in mentioning the circlet. So, Fawn. Where is the circlet?"

"What makes you think I know anything about that?"

Fawn gasped as pain shot through her head and she fell to the floor. Her cheek throbbed, the taste of blood oozing over her tongue. She saw stars amidst a cloud of gray until her vision cleared.

He'd backhanded her, she realized.

Hamstead grabbed her under the arm and yanked her to her feet. She stumbled, swayed, and whimpered as he dragged her from the bedroom. He didn't slow down until he was out of the house, pulling her across the yard as she fought to keep her balance, and through the woods. She tripped over a rock and groaned when she pitched forward, only to have Hamstead's iron grip keep her from hitting the ground. Instead, she felt the pull of muscles in her shoulders as her body twisted until she was able to rectify her position and regain her footing.

"Damn you!"

"I wasn't expecting your mouth, elf. Shut it before I do it for you."

"Like you did Nicholas? And Kalen's mom? Dad?" Fawn worked her jaw for a moment, the ache from his backhand intensifying. Hamstead cast her a cold glance. "How many others have you killed to keep your sick experiments secret? Experiments that you've obviously failed at for years."

Hamstead's lip curled. Fawn wouldn't have been surprised if he sprouted horns and a tail. His fingers tensed around her arm and she braced herself for another attack.

"I have *not* failed, you naïve little creature. I've succeeded in creating a rare crossbreed. A fae and a vampire. That's never been heard of or done before. A vampire who can walk in daylight and has the magic of the fae. A vampire that can possibly destroy one of the most powerful fae races in existence, with a little more tweaking. That is *power*. Power you can only dream of."

She was pushing his buttons, and the brittle tone of his voice warned her to watch her step.

"If that's power, why did you go messing with it when it came to Vivian? Why ruin your *experiment* by injecting something destructive into her?"

"You aren't as smart as I thought."

"Neither are you, apparently."

Fawn squared her shoulders as Hamstead raised his hand to strike her again. She steadily held his gaze. She refused to cower to this beast. That's what he wanted, what he knew, what he craved. If Fawn was anything at all, it certainly wasn't a coward.

Hamstead held his arm up for a long moment, the threat of another blow to her face in his tightly balled fist. His eyes gauged her like a reptile preparing to strike its prey. In those moments, he must've seen her resolve because he sneered, dropped his arm without hitting her, and resumed dragging her through the forest until they reached a black Mercedes SUV with darkly tinted windows.

"You son of a—"

"Do you really think I believed a word you said when I questioned you in your shop?" He snorted out a laugh. "I caught the fear in your eyes when I mentioned Kalen and showed you the picture. I saw you two together. I knew before I stepped foot into your store that you were helping him."

"You've been watching me in my own home?" The idea didn't surprise her as much as it disgusted her.

Oh, that disgust churned her stomach when he flashed her a smile. "What better way to learn a person than in their own environment? Seems Kalen has made your home his own, too."

Hamstead opened the back passenger door with care—such a strange action for someone who gave life so little thought before taking it—and pushed Fawn into the car. He lifted her off her feet before she could dig her heels into the ground and plopped her effortlessly into the seat. She twisted to escape, but earned a painful jab of the gun's muzzle in her ribs.

"Don't try it."

Fawn wanted to spit in his face.

Instead, she let him belt her in, secure her with another modified seatbelt that crossed the first one, then secure her legs with a customized belt from under the seat.

"A luxury paddy wagon, is it?" Fawn asked, unable to resist.

"Luxury for me when I know I have a prize in my backseat." He gave the strap around her knees a brutal tug that forced a gasp from her lungs. His smile was unbearable. "Here's how this is going to work. I will give you two options. You cooperate with the first one, and I won't be forced to use the second."

Hamstead pulled out of the car and opened the front door. Fawn craned her neck to see what he was doing. He didn't make her wait long before brandishing a syringe, filled with a thick yellow substance. She stiffened.

"You will tell me where the circlet is. We will go get it together. I know you have it, but it's not at your house. I've already checked. Jackson was careless in handing it off to you and you were careless in talking about it over the phone."

Fawn mentally smacked herself. She should have suspected Hamstead would have listened to her calls. How that was possible, she hadn't a clue, but the guy had defied most security measures.

"Yes, Fawn. I know you have it. If you decide not to cooperate with me, I will resort to this. It's my very own concoction. It'll turn you into a monster, one programed to destroy vampires. I was going to use it on Vivian the night Nicholas planned the escape. Injected into you? You'll hunt down the vampires and destroy them, if they don't destroy you first. You'll know what you're doing, but you'll have no way of stopping yourself. You'll kill Kalen. You'll kill Vivian. And you will continue to kill. Your vampire friends? Oh, what's her name? Delaney? Yes. That's it."

Fawn simmered in her fury, her breaths sharp and shallow. "You are a *monster*."

Hamstead shrugged. "All in the name of science."

"This isn't science. This is a lust for immorality at its most disgraceful."

"Does that mean you'll cooperate with me?" When Fawn didn't answer—she was too busy grinding her teeth together in impotent fury—Hamstead gave her cheek a friendly pat. "Good. Now, shall we start at that quaint little shop of yours in town?"

Chapter 18

Kalen hesitated when he arrived at Hugh Ellingham's house to find three deputy sheriffs in the front yard. Panic was his first emotion until he overheard one of the deputies say into his cell phone, "No. She didn't return. I'm positive. Delaney was waiting for her. She's not here... No... She knocked him out cold and took off."

Kalen slipped into the shadows of a perfectly trimmed topiary. His attention cut to the driveway. Fear rushed through him when he saw Faunalyn's car missing.

"Alex went to her house. He detected blood in the bedroom..."

Kalen spun away from the house and the activity, and bolted across town to Faunalyn's home. Two deputy sheriffs had taped off the house as a crime scene. Their radios were alive with static talk, all code numbers that made little sense to him. He glided along the shadows, keeping out of the moon's light until he came to the window outside Faunalyn's bedroom. He glanced inside. An officer was on his knees, photographing a splintered area on the floor.

Kalen looked at the desk. The book about the fae was gone.

His mind whirled as he desperately fought to understand what had happened. He needed to know Faunalyn was okay.

"Evidence of one shot fired. The blood isn't from a gunshot wound."

The muffled voice of another officer discussing the scene set off a strange sensation beneath Kalen's skin. He glanced down at his hands to see his skin almost translucent. The moonlight cut across his arm, *through* his arm.

When he looked back into the bedroom, the officers were still there.

But a hazy outline of two other figures was present, too. Their silhouettes shuddered like an old movie reel that kept cutting out. Flashes of their images, bits and pieces of a scene that ultimately left this current scene in its stead.

Hamstead with a gun.

A shot spitting into the floor, right where the corporeal officer snapped an image.

Faunalyn putting gloves on.

Handcuffs.

Hamstead striking Faunalyn, knocking her to the ground.

Nothing.

The figures reappeared, Hamstead dragging Faunalyn out of the bedroom.

Instinctively, Kalen followed along the side of the house, looking in windows, hoping this strange overlap of time didn't cut out for good. If this really happened, if Hamstead found Faunalyn and took her hostage, these fragments were his only lead to finding her.

By the time he reached the front porch, there was nothing.

"If this is my power, if this is my gift, please, help me use it," he whispered to the sky, the universe, hoping by some magic his plea would be heard.

He waited, aware of the movement in the house, keeping his presence hidden. He scanned the yard, the driveway where Faunalyn's car remained parked. He searched for more of the movie…

A disruption of energy drew his attention to the edge of the forest. There, he caught the ghostly appearance of the figures from the house.

Kalen sprinted to them, following a few feet behind as the images faded in and out with faint hisses and sizzles. The interaction between the apparitions was far less active than inside the house, whatever talk they exchanged inaudible.

At last, they arrived at the shadow of a parked Mercedes.

The next frame, Hamstead had Faunalyn strapped into the back seat. He held a syringe in front of her face, the gun at his side.

Kalen caught the steady resolve in Faunalyn's expression, mixed with a powerful hatred for the man in front of her.

Kalen moved between Hamstead and Faunalyn. The doctor stared through him, unaware of his presence. Then again, if Kalen was able to manipulate time and space, he merely watched what had already happened by overlapping the past and the present.

How he was doing it, he didn't know, and he wasn't about to dissect the details. When Faunalyn was safe, he'd study his powers more closely.

He stared at Past Hamstead's mouth, reading his lips as he spoke silently to Faunalyn. His image blacked out, came back, shuddered. Kalen couldn't make sense of the doctor's threat until he reached through Kalen to pat Faunalyn on the cheek.

That's when he swore he recognized the word "shop" on his lips.

The scene disappeared. A surge of heat flooded Kalen's muscles. He tipped his head up to the sky, stared at the moon, and whispered, "Do not abandon me now."

"Damn it, you don't have to rip my shoulder out of my socket!"

Fawn seethed, teeth clenched, the dull throb rolling up from her shoulder where the jerk twisted her arm. He shoved her onto the floor of her office at Magical

Mayhem. Her back hit the front of her desk, a new wave of pain shooting up her back and her head. Geez, when she was through with this ordeal—if she survived it—she was going to treat herself to a spa day to massage all the knots and kinks out of her body, courtesy of the bad doctor.

Hamstead brushed his hands together. Fawn eyed the gun tucked in the holster at his hip. If she had more use of her hands, she'd have lunged for the thing.

"You must have a secret compartment here somewhere. I've checked it out and wasn't able to find anything."

"I don't have it," Fawn said. She couldn't keep the red-hot anger from her voice. It only seemed to please Hamstead.

"You aren't one to trust another with such an important object, are you?"

Fawn shrugged her uninjured shoulder. "Maybe I am. I trust a lot of people in this town."

"I can always make a path through those people, if that's the game you want to play. I don't often leave a trail in my wake."

"Maybe not a trail, but definitely a stench."

"I'll be happy to be rid of you and your wretched mouth."

"Well, until then, I might as well enjoy pissing you off."

Fawn braced herself for another strike as Hamstead pulled back his foot. She hoped his boot was good leather if he was going to make her eat it.

"Hurt her again, and you will not have me."

Fawn's heart stopped. Her head snapped up and she saw Kalen in the doorway, looking more like an ethereal angel than any vampire or fae she'd ever seen. His diamond-crushed blue eyes shimmered with radiant color, almost blinding in their brilliance. His skin was more smoky than firm. His movements trailed a half-second behind his actual body.

Sweet goddess.

Hamstead, eyes wide, stared at Kalen.

Fawn dug her heels into the floor and shoved herself away from the beast. Unfortunately, she wasn't fast enough. Hamstead caught her under her traumatized arm and yanked her to her feet.

"I won't hurt her if you agree to come with me peacefully," Hamstead bartered.

Kalen tilted his head, eyes narrowed. "I can easily free her of you. I'm far faster and far more powerful, now that I'm free of your lab and your drugs."

Fawn stiffened and arched when she felt the stab of the needle in her side. Tears filled her eyes.

"Kalen, don't you give in to him," Fawn warned.

"Where's the circlet, Fawn?" Hamstead hissed against her ear. She felt a sting in her side and knew instantly he had injected her with a warning drop. Kalen stepped closer. "Don't, Kalen. All I have to do is push the plunger and she will become a mercenary at my command. You'll be forced to destroy her if you wish to live."

The devastation that ripped through Kalen's expression tore at her heart. She swallowed the knot in her throat, the rise of regret, the pain of never knowing a life with Kalen. But, whatever the cost, she would make sure he was free.

Her love for him was strong enough for her to accept the sacrifice.

Hamstead shook her. "Where's the circlet?"

"I know where it is." Kalen's gaze shifted to her for a split moment before he set his mask of indifference in place. "I'll come with you voluntarily if you let her go free."

"After you give me the circlet."

Kalen nodded once. Fawn whimpered as she watched, helpless.

"Don't do it, Kalen. Don't…" She squeezed her eyes shut as another burn spread through her side.

She couldn't bear to watch. He couldn't give up his freedom, his sister's freedom. He couldn't hand over the circlet. Not for her.

She listened as he revealed the safe behind the shelves and wall panel. The dial spun and the door clicked open. Hamstead shuffled her away from Kalen, closer to the officer door. She held his wrist to keep the needle from moving.

She opened her eyes as Kalen turned away from the safe, the circlet held at eye-level between his hands. The moonstone glowed as brilliantly as his eyes. The jewels along the golden vine work glittered with unnatural light.

Hamstead's attention shifted from her to the circlet.

Kalen's gaze lowered to her side, then met her eyes. The faintest of grins touched his mouth.

An overwhelming calm came over her. No fear. No panic. Just...calm. A sense of destiny. A trust in fate.

Fawn shoved at the bend of Hamstead's elbow, pulling the needle from her side. She spun out of his grip, catching the flash of movement as Kalen placed the circlet on his head.

"Fool!" Hamstead bellowed.

Fawn ran for the back door, her bound arms making her escape awkward.

She heard the shot ring out.

Felt the punch of the bullet right between her shoulder blades—

Chapter 19

Dead.

She should have been dead.

Not standing in her bedroom, facing Hamstead's gun.

Fawn blinked, a phantom pain in her face, her chest, her shoulder. All of it faded with each second that passed as she tried to catch her breath.

Tried to make sense of what she was seeing.

"What on earth...?" she whispered.

"Don't think I haven't been watching you two. You see, I've had many years to watch him. To learn him. What makes him tick. What makes him retreat. I have the means to make him yield—"

"Sheriff's office! Put the gun down!"

Fawn jumped, eyes wide. Hamstead jerked around as Hank Merrow appeared at the edge of the doorway, gun trained on the mad doctor. Light flashed through her bedroom window and she saw another officer with a rifle pointed in Hamstead's direction.

"Gun! Down!"

Fawn stumbled toward the wall, out of the line of fire, her mind spinning.

"What is happening?"

"Are you okay?"

Arms wrapped around her, pulling her into a hard, familiar body. She fought to breathe, her confusion suffocating. Her hands found Kalen's shoulders and she hung on for dear life. Every inch of her trembled and her knees buckled, but Kalen held her tight, supporting her when she felt she would crumble.

"You're under arrest," Hank snapped at Hamstead.

Alex stepped into her shaky vision, holstering his Glock. "Fawn, we've got him. Are you okay?"

Fawn nodded, unable to speak. She was okay, physically...she thought. But mentally? That was another issue.

"Your friend here was able to tip us off. You know, you should've been at Hugh's."

"I know." The two words sounded more like a squeak. Kalen's arms tightened a little more, and for the first time, she felt a subtle caress of bright warmth along her spirit. His power. She placed her head on his chest and closed her eyes, biting back the sob that tried to emerge. She would *not* cry. "I'm sorry for not listening."

"Had you listened, we might still be looking for this guy. The stars lined up."

"Alex, mind getting him to the cruiser?" Hank asked. Fawn listened to Alex's steps cross the room before she remembered something.

Her eyes snapped open. She searched the floor of her room for the bullet hole.

Her floor was intact.

She looked up at Kalen as Hank joined them.

"Fawn, I'm going to have to ask you some questions," Hank said. His eyes glinted dangerously, a warning that she would most likely face additional scolding for disobeying his orders.

That was okay.

Everything was okay.

Kalen was safe. Vivian was on the road to recovery.

Hamstead was in cuffs and she knew Hank would make sure he never saw the outside of a metal-bar cage again.

The lab would be shut down. No more paranormals would be subjected to the torture of the mad doctor.

"That's fine," Fawn said.

Hank nodded, his attention shifting to Kalen. "Whatever you did, thank you."

"I brought him here. The least I could do was help get him out," Kalen said.

"Well, we'll make sure of that. We need to secure the scene, so I'm going to have to ask you to leave the house for the time being. You can head down to the station. I'll question you there." Hank gave Kalen's shoulder a clap. "Take care of her in the meantime, you hear?"

"You have nothing to worry about."

Fawn allowed Kalen to lead her from her house to her car. Her legs remained weak and shaky, but at least she could stand without the threat of falling over.

"Care to fill me in on what I just experienced?" Fawn asked. "And where's the circlet?"

Kalen reached behind his back and produced the circlet from under his shirt. He flashed her a half-grin, his satisfaction slipping through the seams of his expression. She smiled and shook her head.

"I think I tapped into my powers. Either that, or someone up in the stars heard my plea not to abandon me." Kalen held open the passenger door for her and helped her settle into the seat. He leaned down and pressed a kiss filled with love and relief to her mouth. After that single kiss, she was able to breathe again. "I'll tell you about it on the way to the police station."

And he did.

Fawn listened in awe as he described what he saw at her house, how it led him to her store, and how he followed a newly recognized instinct to warp time and space.

"So, essentially, you manipulated time," Fawn said as Kalen finished his story.

He shrugged. "According to what Jackson told me at Hugh's house, that's part of my power. I don't understand the mechanics of how I activated it, but I'm not going to question it." He lifted her hand and kissed fingertips. "I still have you here, with me. I want you with me forever."

"You think you can handle me?" Fawn laughed softly despite her spirits taking flight.

Kalen laughed as he pulled into the sheriff's department parking lot. "I think that question should be reversed. After all, I believe I wore on your nerves in the beginning."

Fawn waited for him to park before she leaned over and sank her fingers into his soft hair. She didn't care how much the moon enhanced his beauty or how magical his very essence felt. He wanted to be with her, and she'd have it no other way.

"I think that's what made me fall in love with you." She slanted her mouth over his, kissing him with a mixture of relief, tenderness, and need. Kalen groaned against her lips, his arms sliding around her body and pulling her onto his lap. She broke the kiss and let out a happy sigh, perfectly content cradled between the steering wheel and his body. "I wouldn't want you any other way."

"Even though I know so little about this world?"

Fawn traced his brow, then his lips. "I'm going to enjoy the journey teaching you how wonderful this world can be."

"Good, because I don't want anyone else by my side except for you. The woman who taught me the best thing I've learned so far." He kissed the tip of her nose. "How wonderful love is."

Chapter 20

One Month Later

"Welcome to Magical Mayhem, where we are more than just smoothies!"

Kalen chuckled at his sister's greeting to the customers. He listened from the back office as he finished dealing with the last of the invoices. He basked in this newly acquired freedom, not having to worry about danger and threats and Vivian's health. Hugh's remedy had worked, along with Faunalyn's magical touch, and Vivian was virus-free. He couldn't describe how relieved he was to see his sister regain her flare for life as her body healed.

She was beyond excited to be part of Faunalyn's business. Her eagerness to help customers was contagious. The customers enjoyed her charisma, and it filled Kalen with more pride to watch her flourish in this new world.

He had learned a tremendous amount of valuable information over the last few weeks. Hugh explained how vampires were made—a three-bite process—but warned him not to try it with Faunalyn for fear it would kill her. He swore off the prospect. They would both live long lives together. He didn't need to make a vampire out of her, although he had taken her up on her offer to occasionally drink from her vein. He didn't possess the willpower to decline such a precious gift.

Faunalyn and her friends, residents who had taken him and Vivian in without hesitation, taught them the ins and outs of Nocturne Falls. He learned about the magical water the tourists drank that came from a waterfall in the forest. Somehow, it made it difficult for humans to tell the difference between the real and the unreal. He was reassured that around the full moon, he didn't have to hide because of the way his skin or eyes appeared. In fact, Julian Ellingham encouraged him to use his roots to add a bit of flare to the town at night.

Faunalyn later suggested he ignore Julian's advice. He had to agree with his beloved.

Jackson shared Nicholas's final letter with Kalen and Vivian. It ended up being more of a small book than a simple letter. The details of the siblings' fae lineage, as well as their vampire bloodline, was enlightening. His mother had shared far more details about tapping into his power and his magic than anyone expected. He learned just how important the circlet was to this power, especially here on Earth. The circlet belonged to him, as per the laws of Celestial succession, but he planned to share it with his sister so they could learn the foundation of their magic together.

In addition to the history lesson, Nicholas disclosed the bank accounts that their parents had set up. Kalen was shocked by the sudden wealth.

Although he had split the funds down the middle with his lovely sister, he was frugal. He and Faunalyn decided to keep the funds for emergency use only, and they would work for a living.

He loved this work.

He loved this life.

He loved the woman who showed him promise and trust and love in return.

"Knock knock."

Kalen looked up from the desk. Jackson pushed his glasses up onto the bridge of his nose—it seemed they were always falling down—and waved. Kalen motioned for him to come in as he leaned back in his chair.

"Hope I'm not interrupting."

Kalen shook his head. "Never. Do tell. Is everything set?"

Jackson took a seat across from Kalen and smiled. He stretched out his legs and dug a hand into the pocket of his jeans. Kalen's heart thumped when he saw the ornate wooden box with the small gold clasp. Jackson placed it on the desk in front of Kalen.

"Willa did a damn fine job on that piece."

Kalen flicked his fingers. The box opened magically. Nestled in the bed of velvet, the vision of a promised forever.

"Yes. Yes, she did." Kalen closed the lid with the same magic and tucked the box into his jacket pocket. "Are you planning to stay and help Vivi and Wendy close up the shop?"

"Of course. I wouldn't leave her alone."

Kalen grinned. The last month and a half had created a deeply woven bond between the nephew of Kalen's first true friend and he and Vivian. There were times the young man definitely worked his last nerve, but in the end, he and Jackson knew the lengths each would go to save the other.

"Then I should take off." Kalen neatened the papers on the desk and stood up. "Thank you, Jackson."

"I'd better see you two tomorrow."

Kalen laughed as he stepped into the front of the store. Vivian flashed him a bright smile as she handed a smoothie to a customer. Wendy wiggled her fingers in hello as she topped a granola bowl with fruit.

"Are you leaving?" Vivian asked. He kissed her tenderly on the forehead.

"Jackson will help you close up so you ladies aren't alone. I want to get back home before Faunalyn arrives." He glanced at his watch. "And I have to pick up dinner from Café Claude."

"You need to learn to cook."

"I'm working on that. Have a good night and I'll see you in the morning."

Vivian pecked his cheek one last time before she returned to her customers.

Kalen rushed to Café Claude to pick up the food he had ordered and hurried to get home before Faunalyn arrived from her girls' night out. He adored her friends and their excitement and willingness to get her out of the area so he could set up this special night.

He'd learned quickly that Georgian summers were torture, but he refused to bring dinner inside. Instead, he used his newly found magic to create a comfortable temperature around the back patio. Candles and wine and gourmet cuisine. He touched the moonflower plants that surrounded the patio, unleashed the nighttime magic to unfurl their soft white petals.

And not a moment too soon.

Headlights coasted through the trees as Faunalyn's ride approached the house. He took the next few minutes to slip into a fresh shirt, brush back his hair, and meet his beloved at the front door.

The look of delight on her face when she realized he was home early was all he needed. She waved to Ivy and Bridget before stepping into the house, closing the door, and greeting him with one world-tilting kiss. A kiss that left him catching her as she hopped up, wrapped her legs around his waist, and threatened to break every last shred of his strength.

"You look so handsome," she murmured against his mouth, then giggled. "I couldn't help myself."

Kalen chuckled. "You can do that all you want. But I have a surprise for you."

Faunalyn perked up, her brows lifting. Her golden hair caressed her cheeks with satin waves, highlighting the lavender and gold hue of her eyes. He was a sucker for her little red dress and how it showed off every delectable curve of her body.

"Surprise?"

"Come."

Faunalyn slid back to her feet, her hand slipping into his. He led her to the patio, admiring her deepening blush as she soaked in the dinner laid out for them.

"I hope you didn't eat much."

Faunalyn shook her head and accepted the seat he pulled out for her. "Thank you. Actually, I'm starving. Those women know how to keep you running."

"Are you sure you weren't doing the running?"

"To keep up with them, yes." She kicked up her feet. "My legs are short."

Kalen laughed, trailing a hand over her bare leg as he moved to his chair. She lowered her feet to the ground. "Your legs are perfect. So is your waist, and your chest, and everything about you."

"Are you trying to woo your way into my bed again?"

Kalen settled into his chair and popped the cork from the wine bottle. "I've wooed you every night so far, haven't I?"

"Without a doubt."

He poured her a glass of wine. "By the greeting I received at the door, I don't think I'll have much work to do. However, that's for later." Kalen poured himself a glass and set the bottle on the table. He lifted his glass. "To you, beloved Faunalyn. For being the amazing woman you are and for putting up with me."

"I deserve that toast," she teased, tapping the lip of her glass to his. He chuckled. "I put up with a lot from you. All of your hugs and kisses."

"Touché."

"New word?"

Kalen snorted. "Not quite. I recall hearing it from you."

The teasing continued over dinner. It never got old. The comfort they shared was a blessing he cherished. Every minute with Faunalyn was a sacred gift, one he would never give up for the world. Or, in this instance, the universe. Although he had yet to meet one of the Celestial fae, he was perfectly content with his choices for this life, a life only complete with the golden-haired, fiery elf sharing dinner with him beneath the moon.

"That was fantastic," Faunalyn said, dabbing the napkin at the corner of her mouth. She leaned back in her chair and watched him with adoration in her eyes. "Thank you for a beautiful night."

Kalen took a sip of his wine. He hadn't expected his nerves to rattle as his planned moment came upon him.

"You're very welcome." He climbed to his feet and gathered the finished plates. "Stay here, my darling. I'll be right back."

Faunalyn reached for his arm as he rounded her chair. Her head leaned back and she looked up at him, her eyes sparkling and her hair falling down the back of the chair like a golden waterfall. The moon adored her complexion and teased him with shadows leading down the fine swells of cleavage into her dress.

"A kiss?"

How could he not?

He leaned over and pressed a lingering kiss to her lips.

"Let me put these in the kitchen." He shook the desire away long enough to make it to the kitchen, retrieve the box from the top of the fridge, and return to the patio.

He found Faunalyn caressing moonflower petals.

"These are beautiful, Kalen."

"I figured you'd appreciate them, with your love of flowers."

She glanced over her shoulder. "You know me well."

"I'd like to think so." He approached her, keeping his hands behind his back. "But there is still much I believe I have to learn about you."

She turned to face him, her smile serene. "What would you like to know?"

Kalen moistened his lips. She couldn't have opened the door for him any more perfectly.

He lowered to one knee and presented her with the box. Her eyes went wide and her hands flew to her mouth.

And in a snap, he forgot the speech he prepared.

Seconds passed and he choked on his words until he managed to say, "I would love for you to want to spend the rest of your life with me."

The top of the box opened.

Faunalyn's eyes shimmered with tears when she met his gaze. He could smell the salt and hear the shuddered breaths.

"I want nothing more—"

"Yes!"

His brows furrowed. "Yes?"

Faunalyn tugged at his arm until he stood up. She threw her arms around his neck and kissed him until he nearly forgot himself.

When she pulled back, cheeks streaked with tears, she nodded vigorously. "Yes, Kalen. Yes, yes, and yes again. I'll spend the rest of *eternity* with you."

Kalen pulled the ring from the box. "Then I guess I should make it official, huh?"

He took her left hand and slid the gold band set with an oval moonstone flanked by diamonds on Faunalyn's finger. Willa had fashioned the ring after his circlet, and the similarities were stunningly close.

"It's beautiful," Faunalyn breathed.

"Almost as beautiful as the woman who owns my heart." Kalen wrapped his arms around her waist and drew her close. "Now, about that wooing."

Faunalyn laughed, her fingers gliding into his hair as she pulled his head down to hers. "Silly man. You still have so much to learn." She teased him with an airy brush of her lips. "But tonight is for us."

The End

About Kira Nyte

Born and raised a Jersey girl with easy access to NYC, I was never short on ideas for stories. I started writing when I was 11, and my passion for creating worlds exploded from that point on. Romance writing came later, since kissing gave you cooties at 11, but when it did, I embraced it. Since then, all of my heroes and heroines find their happily ever after, even if it takes a good fight, or ten, to get there.

I currently live in Central Florida with my husband, our four children, and two parakeets. I work part-time as a PCU nurse when I'm not writing or traveling between sports and other activities.

I love to hear from readers!
Contact me at kiranyteauthor@gmail.com

Made in the USA
Middletown, DE
13 August 2018